The Eridanos Library 10

# Giuseppe Pontiggia

# The Invisible Player

Translated by Annapaola Cancogni

Eridanos Press

# The Invisible Player

I

On a bright and blustery morning, as he held on to
his hat with one hand and to his briefcase with the
other and peered through the glare of his glasses at the
distant figure of his assistant scurrying toward him
across the university square, the professor knew something was amiss.

He found shelter by a concrete sentry-box and decided
not to budge until the other had reached him. The
assistant was waving a magazine in his hand, but the
professor could not see what it was until it got closer:
*The Voice of Antiquity*. The young man handed it to
him.

"I hope you won't mind it, sir."

"Mind what?" the professor asked, popping his
eyes.

"A lowdown slander."

"Come, come," the professor said. "Not here."

They hastened along the walk that led to the main
hall, passed under the dark vaults of the vestibule,

where someone greeted the professor, emerged under the colonnade of the cloister, and crossed the court diagonally. Then they took staircase C, between dirty flaking walls. When they turned into the corridor with low windows and a glistening marble floor, the assistant slowed down to wait for the professor who had lagged a few steps behind. Sunlight played between their feet. The corridor was empty, the street noise reached them muffled by distance.

A blast of wind greeted them as they entered the office. The window had been burst wide open. As the assistant rushed to close it, the professor sat down in his chair and passed a hand over his face.

"Forget about them," he said, gesturing toward the papers scattered all over the floor. "Let me read this."

"Yes, sir. It's a letter in the *Touché* column."

"It's a frivolous column. The first thing one reads."

"Here. Page 82," and with his index finger, the assistant drew the professor's attention to a line close to the top margin. "This is where it begins."

The professor started to read.

Hypocrisy is the water in which we all swim: it keeps us afloat all our lives, and, in the end, sinks us. But if we know the essence of hypocrisy ("A glance is enough, you know what I mean") what do we know of the word's origins? An expert on the subject (of hypocrisy, that is) reveals them to us in a column he now edits for a popular magazine—maybe in the hope of expanding his readership beyond the realm of scholardom, maybe, more banally (and, therefore, more probably), for lucrative reasons. But this only concerns him, him and the dreams of cultural omnipotence that have befogged his

4

mind since the years, alas remote, of his academic debut. On the other hand, there is something that we ought not to overlook, and this is the nonchalance with which he eludes and distorts the acquisitions of philological science, thus sowing error among his hapless readers. A complete list of all such improprieties would require too much time and space, we shall therefore limit it to two pearls:

"*Hypocrite*, from Latin *hypocrita*, from Greek hypokrités"

no problem so far; but let's proceed:

"from the verb *hypokrínesthai*, meaning to *dissemble*."

Is it possible to commit a more unbelievable howler? In Homer, the verb has two basic meanings: 1) to interpret, 2) to answer. Only later, when tragedy was born, did the term "hypocrite" start to indicate "he who *answers* to the chorus." The passage from the meaning of "actor" to that of "dissembler" took place yet later when the term was no longer used to indicate one who plays a part on the stage, but one who plays a part in the reality of life.

One more mishap concerns the meaning of "hypocrite" in the Greek of the New Testament:

"Woe unto you, scribes and Pharisees, hypocrites!" *Matthew 23.* Here "hypocrites" does not merely mean "dissemblers"; as has been exhaustively demonstrated (by Zucchelli among others), it also means men in "objective" contradiction with themselves, which is why Christ also calls them "fools and blind." But will our friend be able to see the difference?

Convinced that in scholarship "two plus two

equals four," our humanist is at peace with himself. But in reality, two plus two does not necessarily equal four. Life is full of surprises, particularly for those who don't expect them. As a matter of fact, we are probably surprising him right now, which is partly why we have decided to write this, so as to eliminate any doubt from the outset. After all, he should realize there is still time to mend one's ways. Meanwhile, he can also ponder over this definition by Theophilattus: "A hypocrite is one thing but seems another."

*Name and Address withheld*

The professor started wheezing.

"Do you have any idea who it could be?" the assistant asked him.

"No."

The professor's hands were clutching the edge of his desk.

"Are you going to reply?"

"No," he said. "It would be a mistake to give him elbow room."

At the ten o'clock bell, the assistant quietly left the office. Sidling along the walls, he avoided two groups of students and bowed to Salutati. The professor of romance philology was standing in the bay of a mullioned window, slouched in weary pinguidity. He responded to the bow with a vague smile and then beckoned to him faintly with his hand. The assistant promptly crossed the corridor.

"How are you, Professor?"

"Fine, my dear. Fine. Can't you see?" The complacency with which he enunciated every word brimmed with maliciously elusive allusions. "And what about

6

you? Tell me. I know you made a splash with your adjectives ending in *bundus.*"

"Why, sir! What did you hear?"

"Only good things," Salutati answered. "It's a shame I should have been bedridden in a hospital while you were giving your talk at the Classics' Circle."

"It will come out as a booklet before the end of the year," the assistant told him. "Did they tell you about the little barb I aimed at you?"

Surprised, Salutati moved away from the mullioned window, and bent forward, ever so slightly.

"No," he said. "What was it?"

"Nothing much, Professor. Something to do with *muribundus* in Statius."

"Of course," Salutati said. "They did mention something of the sort. But, am I wrong or was my research somewhat myopic?"

"That was precisely the gist of my criticism, sir."

"Good," Salutati exclaimed. "Any young man who wants to get ahead should be ruthless. Even if it means," and he raised the index finger of his bejewelled hand, "going up *against* his own teachers."

He went on:

"Woe to the pupil who does not outdo his master. By the way, what about yours? Is he still sitting on you, still keeping you from taking wing?"

The assistant smiled but did not answer.

"How is he?"

"He is fine."

"This morning he looked a little peaked. Any problem? Clouds on the horizon?"

The assistant lowered his eyes.

"You know how emotional he is," he said.

"Indeed, much too much. Could it have anything to do with that short piece in *The Voice of Antiquity?*"

7

"When did you see it?"

"Easter eve," Salutati said. "An egg with a little surprise in it, or, if you prefer, a little surprise with no egg."

The assistant smiled and glanced down into the yard.

"I hope that's not the reason," Salutati said. "A man of his stature should be above such things."

He pulled a silver cigarette case out of his vest pocket.

"Of course," he added. "One can't say it isn't nasty. Deftly done, but unsigned. That's its weakness."

"Its greatest weakness."

"Yes," Salutati said, "since the rest is quite convincing. Misleadingly so, as we all know."

At that very moment the professor emerged from his office. When he saw the two of them at the end of the corridor he feigned forgetfulness and retreated back inside.

"I must leave you now, Professor," the assistant said.

"Yes, my dear."

The assistant started toward the staircase but, turning around, he saw that the professor had again come out of his office. He caught up with him in mid-corridor.

"Aren't you going to correct the exams, Professor?"

"No."

As he kept on walking, he added:

"You go ahead."

"Are you all right, Professor?"

"Yes. I'm perfectly fine."

Salutati's voice reached them from their left.

"Good morning, old boy!"

8

Touching his hat, the professor nodded and immediately turned toward the staircase.

"I'll see you tomorrow," he told the assistant as soon as they had reached the first landing.

"Don't you want me to walk with you?"

"No, thank you."

Two steps down, he stopped and, with his hand on the banister, turned around.

"Better not mention it."

"What?"

"The article. Better let it self-destruct."

"All right, Professor. I won't mention it to anybody."

"Just make sure you don't mention it to everybody."

He leaned against the banister.

"I'm afraid of the way these things tend to get out of hand," he added. "I hate personal polemics."

"Excuse my saying so, Professor," the assistant said stepping down to the other's level, "but you're also quite critical of your colleagues."

"But never on a personal level. Only on a scientific level."

"True."

"Anyway," the professor said. His eyes glinted in the shadows. "Enough of it. Let's consider the subject closed."

But when, back in the windy square, his briefcase slipped from under his arm as he was holding on to his hat and he became aware of the chilly stares from a group of students, he knew the subject was far from closed.

Who could it be? Salutati? He remembered seeing him, one evening before the Christmas holidays, under the arcades: he was wearing a fur hat and, his hands clasped behind his back, was staring at two hamsters in the window of a pet-shop. He had touched his shoulder and Salutati, only half-straightening his back, had told him:

"Look at them, it's very instructive." Taking his arm, he had added: "They were born yesterday. But their mother is no longer with them. You know why?"

"She died."

"No, my dear. Are you really unable to guess? You of all people?"

He had slowly pushed him toward the center of the arcades in the direction of a bar.

"The mother gives birth to them and then eats them," he had continued. "Which is exactly what you'd like to do to your students."

And when he had told him that the comparison was absurd:

"Maybe so," Salutati had answered. "But I like absurd ideas. They are the most fruitful. Invention means reviving, as you once pointed out to me."

"What are you driving at?" he had asked him.

"Oh, nothing, really," Salutati had answered. "But let me give you an example. If you believe in something, then the opposite is true. Take my word, it's a very useful precept, even in a relationship, even with friends."

While talking he had slipped his gloves on.

"If you believe a friend loves you," he had continued, "well, then you must convince yourself of the opposite, that he hates you. You'll see how well it works."

Inside the bar, he had looked at him as if he were seeing him for the first time. His eyes betrayed cold curiosity.

"Would you like something warm to drink?" he had asked him.

"It's him," the professor said half aloud.

Staggering under a sudden onrush of fear that sapped him of his energy, he stopped in the middle of the square and closed his eyes. Where was Salutati now? When he reopened his eyes, the university was again in front of him. He made his way through flights of pigeons and soon found himself in the main hall and then in the cloister. As he climbed staircase C, he missed a step but managed to break his fall by hanging on to the banister. He stood up, looked around, and started climbing the steps more slowly, his head held high. But Salutati was not by the mullioned window. Elbows resting on a table, hands cupping a perfectly bald head, a janitor was absorbed in a newspaper.

"Have you seen Professor Salutati?"

"He was here just a little while ago. I think he's meeting with his students in the Quintiliano lecture room," and the janitor pointed across the courtyard.

But in the Quintiliano lecture room, at the bottom of the well-lit amphitheater with just a few students scattered here and there along the farthest tiers, he saw no Salutati. At his place was Paolucci, the professor of Greek grammar, as pale and spare as ever. With a shrill voice and the tip of his left thumb pressed against that of his left index finger, he was enunciating:

*kókkyx*
*kókkygos*

The professor quietly closed the door and wiped the sweat off his brow. Then, he removed his glasses,

11

cleaned them, pointed them against the sun, and, suddenly, in a halo of flashing light, saw Salutati behind the panes of a second floor window. He immediately waved at him, but his colleague moved away. He crossed the yard, climbed the main staircase, emerged under the glassed-in gallery, but it was empty. He opened the only door on his left and found himself facing a row of white sinks. Coming out, he bumped into a student.

"Have you seen Professor Salutati?"

"No, I haven't, Professor," the student answered, taken aback.

As he continued on, he felt his face flush. He walked to the end of the hallway, then down the cast-iron steps of staircase B, into an iridescent cylinder of frosted glass, and, wrapping his black overcoat tight against himself, emerged under the colonnade of the cloister. Here, his heartbeat slowed down. What if it weren't Salutati? Whom could he ask? Someone who knew everybody and was nobody's friend. Martelli.

Back in the main hall, he turned left and, at the top of three steps, opened a small wooden door that led into the old Varrone lecture room, now a storage room for printed matter. He walked along dusty shelves and, at the bottom of the steps leading to the emergency exit, turned into a long and narrow passage whose walls were lined with fragments of Roman memorial stones, busts, and stone pots. Beyond the yellowed panes and the bars, he could see the janitor's garden at the bottom of the moat. Where the passage forked, an arrow pointed in the direction of the library, to the right. He climbed a few steps, pushed open the swing door and found himself right behind the editor-in-chief.

Seated in his chair, motionless and stiff-necked in his high collar, Martelli was staring straight ahead, the palms of his hands spread on his glass-topped desk. Editor-in-chief of the literary journal *New Narrative*, he used to screen the manuscripts he received with a rigor as intense as the secret confusion he felt every time he came across some unknown author. Affable, polite, imperturbable, he would sometimes ask for the opinions of his editors and was perfectly capable of changing his own, had he not already expressed them. Once expressed, however, his opinions were inflexible. A slight contraction of his pupils behind his glasses bespoke the complacency of academic neutrality and the superiority of firm conviction. He was accused of being too partial to his own errors, but the editor-in-chief maintained that he couldn't possibly be partial to any opinion since he had none; rather, he was seduced by the hypothesis of an opinion, and remained faithful to it to the end. This abstract coherence had helped him best his more impulsive competitors and had kept him, or rather, had confirmed him in a coveted post.

Reflected in the desk-top glass, Martelli stiffly turned his head, and, with an angular Adam's apple protruding from his thin neck, said in a conventionally affable tone of voice:

"Hello."

And, after a pause:

"Why did you come in the side door?"

"I didn't feel like greeting them," the professor answered, gesturing toward the bowed heads and pensive noses in the reading room, beyond the glass partition.

"We are so different," Martelli said. "Other people don't even exist for me."

13

"I know, you have already told me that. But I need to ask you something."

He drew a wicker chair up to the corner of the desk and, sitting down, asked him:

"If you had to name one of my enemies out there, who would it be?"

"Among the people in the reading room?" Martelli asked staring at the glass partition.

"No, in general, on campus."

"Carulli."

"Carulli?"

"Yes."

"Why Carulli?"

Martelli turned his head toward him:

"I've heard him express some reservations."

"About what?"

"Obviously, I cannot go into the details," Martelli answered. "Your style, for instance. He finds you, how shall I put it?" He closed his eyes. "A bit too fluent."

"Tell me what was the expression he used, exactly."

"It's a bit vulgar, at least for my tastes. He says you have a leaky quill. . ."

"A what?"

"I think he means a glib pen. But, please, don't take it like that. Besides, I don't think he is the only one."

Blushing, the professor looked at him. After a pause, he asked:

"He's not the only one of that opinion?"

"Of course not. What did you expect?"

The professor answered with tight lips:

"That they would say those things to my face, not behind my back."

"Fine," Martelli said. "On the other hand, you have to admit, not everybody can afford to be honest. What about those who don't have the courage of their opinions?"

"I have the feeling you are hiding something from me."

Suddenly, Martelli's eyes turned glassy.

"Let's say that you have asked me for my opinion, and that I have given it to you," he answered. "In fact, it would be best if you acted as if I hadn't said a thing."

He pulled his gold watch out of his breast pocket and pressed its crown.

"I'm very sorry, but I must go now," he said. "I'm expected upstairs," he pointed toward the ceiling, "at the Restoration Center. Goodbye." He took his leave with the same calm tone of voice with which he had greeted him a few minutes earlier. "You know where to find me."

He left through the Renaissance door at the other end of the reading room, the one over which was inscribed: *"È bello doppo il morire vivere anchora."*

The professor remembered a morning in July, a walk along the lake right below Villa Strinati, where the Linguistics Convention was taking place, and Carulli inviting him to run away, as he pointed toward the shimmering lake-dwellings, among the rushes on the opposite bank:

"What would you say to an escape into the neolithic?"

And yet, when Carulli had shown up, three quarters of an hour late, his white hat alone visible above the railway station fence, he had greeted him with harsh words, causing Carulli to shrink from him with a bewildered look. From that moment on, Carulli had avoided him, just as he avoided all his other col-

15

leagues. The twenty years he had been waiting to get a part-time position at the university had burnt him out. Still unsure, at forty-five, whether to consider himself a teacher or a student, he would roam the corridors, feverish and furtive, as swift in his greetings as in his exits, constantly shying away from contact, limp-handed, sarcastic during exams, and yet intolerant of the hostility he seemed to elicit. He imagined Carulli creeping by a building in the snow, jerky, terrified. He saw himself finally catching up with him, and pushing him against the wall to make him confess everything. But at that very moment he realized that it was all a misunderstanding: he saw Carulli slump down into the snow and vanish, while he sat motionless, in the room, casting about for a name.

He stood up and walked to the bookcase along the right wall, where the periodicals were kept under glass. The ones devoted to the classics, lined up along a slanted shelf, as if resting on a lectern, had their first issues on display in the darkest corner. He pressed a button on the side of the bookcase, and the covers beneath the glass immediately glimmered in the light: *East and West* with Odysseus' raft floating on a golden sea; *Apollon*'s sun with rays like Medusa's hair; *Græcia*'s Parthenon frieze midst Liberty tendrils twining around a Doric capitol; *Minerva's Owl* glowering at the reader from its perch, followed by the beheaded column of *Philologica;* the lizard crawling over the broken mosaic of *Trinacria; Hesperia*'s golden apple hanging on a branch; the dolphin flipping over a wave of *Mare Nostrum;* the curve of Olympia's stadium on *Hellas' Youth;* the Latian ox of *Origines;* a flight of falcons over the head of *Etruria*'s editor-in-chief; the glossy cover of *Muses;* the tunnel in the cyclopic walls of *Italic Antiquities;* and, finally, the tragic mask, in India ink, of *The Voice of Antiquity,* with its gaping mouth beneath two empty eye sockets. At the bottom of the cover it said: "founded in the fifth year of the Unification." That's when he saw the assistant warily enter the room through the other door, over which was inscribed *"Silentium."* He was walking across the light streaming in through the window, and, having reached the bookcase with the journals, stretched his thin arms toward the top shelf and delicately grasped a few issues of *The Voice of Antiquity.* As he was pulling out the journals, his eyes met those of the professor, on the other side of the glass. He immediately put the journals back onto the shelf and made his way toward him, gracefully negotiating the intervening desks and chairs.

"Are you looking for something, Professor?"

"No, I am not. And you, what are you looking for?"

"Oh, nothing serious. An essay by Natali on mosaic techniques."

The professor pointed him toward the appropriate shelf, in the center of the reading room.

"What does *The Voice of Antiquity* have to do with it?"

"Ah, you saw me," the assistant nodded. "Right. I wasn't sure whether I should tell you. I wanted to check out the article attacking you. I wanted to compare it with different articles in other issues to see whether I could recognize the author's style."

"But it is not an article."

"Well," the assistant shrugged his shoulders. "Not in the strict sense of the term. But everybody knows they write their own letters."

"Who?"

"The editors. I think a comparison might be revealing. The same words, the same turns of phrase. We are always betrayed by our own language, don't you agree?"

The professor was staring at him.

"I don't know," the assistant went on euphorically. "Maybe I am not making any sense. Really. You tell me."

He leaned against the wall, by the window. The professor kept staring at him.

"What in the world are you doing?" he finally asked him. "Why look for the author? Then the whole thing will snowball, assume gigantic dimensions."

"Yes, Professor."

The professor raised his voice:

"It's worse than anonymity."

"That's true, Professor. But it was also a matter of curiosity. Very trivial, I admit. Very trivial."

The professor remained silent. The heard the arm of the clock clicking to the next minute.

"You understand, I'm not looking for trouble," the professor began, breathing with increasing difficulty. "But if someone attacks me, if someone challenges me," and he grabbed the assistant's arm, "I don't pull back."

"And then, you see," he continued, with a flushed face, "then there is trouble for everybody!" He struck the desk with his hand. "No one can stop me."

"Yes, Professor."

The assistant had lowered his eyes.

"I was only doing it out of curiosity," he added. "Nothing more. If you are interested, I can tell you what I've come up with."

"No!" the professor retorted popping his eyes. "Can't you see it does not interest me? I would have already forgotten everything if you hadn't brought it up again."

"I am sorry, sir."

The assistant kept staring at the floor.

"I must get going, now," he said. "So long, Professor."

As he eased himself into an armchair, the professor saw him, lean and sinewy, steal away through the reading room and disappear. When he got up, his legs felt heavy. Tense, tired, stunned, he retraced his steps through the passage and under the colonnade of the cloister. Then he passed in front of Cicero's statue and turned toward the sunlit square.

## II

He could have never guessed, at the moment when, having laid his hat on the chair in the hallway and removed his glasses, he had casually glanced at the nude etching on the wall and had only seen a smudged outline, at that very moment he could have never guessed what was happening to his wife in the bedroom. But even had he walked around the house and approached the window of their bedroom, even had he flattened his body against the wall beside the sill, and clung to the stucco with the palms of his hands, and craned his neck toward the casing, and peered into the room like a thief who wants to see without being seen, he still would not have understood what was going on. But even had he remained at home, sitting at his desk under his lamp and poring over the *Glossarium Mediae et Infimae Latinitatis*—even then he would not have noticed what was happening behind his back. His wife, seated on the edge of the bed, was on the phone. But even she did not know what was happening. Only if in place of her husband there had been another man, and they had gone to a bar together, and he, smiling at her because he had known her since their childhood, had gently, but firmly, asked her:

"Has it been going on for a long time?" only in that case would she have been delighted to answer:

"Yes."

And if he, the other man, still pursuing the subject as they left the bar and strolled under the arcades, had asked her:

"Have you already been with him?"

"Yes," she would have lied, looking straight into his eyes and blushing.

At which point, without flinching, he would have simply asked:

"What about your husband."

"He still does not suspect anything."

And if, at the end of the arcades, waiting for the traffic light to change, he had paused for a while and then had added: "It had to happen sooner or later," she might have even been able to disagree and feign anger at his refusal to believe her.

Then, as they crossed the street and he squeezed her arm in a sign of complicity, she could have admitted a few more things. And maybe, in the middle of the square, in front of the cathedral, he, suddenly looking at her, would have found her completely transformed (everybody had already noticed it), and she would have enthusiastically said:

"Yes."

Then his questions ought to have become more pressing, thus multiplying all the doubts she could no longer answer, as she stood reflected in the mirror of the hallway, or sat, motionless, in the bedroom, basking in the warm light that filtered in through the

22

window, listening to the dog running on the gravel of the garden. Then, he would have had to look for the answers himself, so as to allow her to go on deferring them and keeping her options open.

But nobody had gone on a walk with her that morning, and her husband still didn't suspect a thing. So she got up from the bed and, walking into the hallway, asked him:

"How come you are back so early this morning?"

"I will tell you later. Would you please make me a cup of tea?"

Sitting in an armchair, his hands on the armrests, the professor loosened his tie and, closing his eyes, let himself sink into a darkness spangled with luminous dots until he found himself inside the large wooden cylinder of an amusement park, its floor and walls already starting to rotate. He wanted to shout for someone to stop the thing, but his body was slowly sucked against the wall. He raised his head, and remained paralyzed in that position. And, while the spectators, who looked in from the rim, were laughing and spinning in the opposite direction with the sky and the trees, he felt the floor slip away from under his feet and he was left spread-eagled on the wall. With a gaping mouth and outspread hands, he thought: "The worst is yet to come." But at that very moment he managed to turn his face and, by and by, to detach a hand from the wooden wall, pushing against the air that had now become as heavy as water. When the cylinder started slowing down, and the crown of spectators became again a circle of heads, he felt he was coming loose, like a fruit, and he crumpled onto the rising floor. There, on all fours, he saw that the others were also dropping to the ground. Then, staggering, they all walked toward the exit. Only then did he realize that they were all young. At the top of the iron staircase that circled the exterior wall of the cylinder, a janitor grabbed him by the shoulder and asked him:

"How old are you?"

"Fifty."

Then he was violently pushed down the steps, and as he was slowly tumbling in the void, his hat flew up, farther and farther away, until it became a small dot and eventually disappeared. Now he was walking through a railway station under luminous glass arcades, among huge black locomotives, still and shiny and as unreal as those of a painting. A ticket collector left his booth and started walking toward him on the deserted platform.

"We know what you are looking for and we have found it," he told him. "Would you be so kind as to follow me."

Deeply touched, he thanked him, but the other did not turn around. He could only see his profile under the cap.

"Don't worry," the other said. "We have found the solution."

They went down a huge staircase. High above it, very large skylights let a yellow light filter into a strange nineteenth-century setting. As they walked on the mosaic floor of the Lost and Found Office, the ticket collector turned toward him:

"I know you are in a hurry," he said. "We won't waste any time."

He bent toward an arched window:

"The gentleman is in a hurry," he said. "Could you please give me the last issue of *The Voice of Antiquity*?"

A hand pushed a sealed envelope through the window. The ticket collector gave it to the professor who asked him:

"What about the other copies?"

"They have all been destroyed, sir, along with the printing plates. Otherwise what would happen to its market value? This is the only extant copy."

He nodded without saying a word, and the ticket collector went on:

"There is an unsigned piece of great value in the column titled *Touché*. Do you know who wrote it?"

"No."

"You don't want to tell us, Professor, but we already know."

He raised his face:

"Really?"

"Of course. So, Professor, why not tell us who wrote it."

"Who wrote it?"

"You wrote it, isn't that so?"

"Of course," he answered, smiling, as if he were only now remembering. "It's true, I wrote it."

Invaded by a great peace, he walked toward the multicolored square, sparkling with cabs under the blue sky, and saw his wife waiting for him at the bus stop, and heard her telling him something that he could not understand, and then she repeated it, with a flat voice. Slowly, she told him:

"It's amazing how frequently you've been falling asleep lately."

To wake up at home, with his wife addressing him from another armchair, was very painful to the professor. He covered his eyes with his hands and then let them slide along his cheeks.

"Can you tell me what is the matter with you?" his wife asked him.

He looked at her in silence.

"Is it something I've done?"

"No."

"Did you hear something when you came in?"

"No. Why?"

She lowered her head. He asked her:

"What was I supposed to have heard?"

"Nothing."

She was smiling, staring at the floor.

"So, you probably were on the phone."

"Yes."

"With whom?"

"With an ex-student of yours."

She raised her head and, looking at him, added:

"Ricci."

"I see! Why did he call you?"

She hesitated for a second and then answered:

"He calls quite often."

"Really?"

"Yes."

"He is a good student, but not altogether convincing," the professor said, getting up. "Aside from the fact that he is a little too effeminate."

She colored with disbelief:

"You really think so?"

"Look, if you want to make me jealous you should not start with someone like him."

He stood up and, walking toward his desk, added:

"And this is not the best time."

He pulled *The Voice of Antiquity* out of his briefcase and handed it to her:

"Have a look at page 82."

While his wife, holding the magazine on her knees, was reading in her armchair, the professor walked to the kitchen and drank a glass of water. Then, he turned around and watched her from a distance. Suddenly, she stopped reading:

"What a bastard!"

"Go on."

She straightened the magazine on her knees and went on. When she was done, she raised her eyes:

"Is this true?"

"Is what true?"

"What the letter says."

The professor put the glass down by the sink.

"You are the first person to put that question to me."

"Well, maybe I was not expressing myself correctly," she justified herself, embarrassed. "But this is not the main point."

She was looking straight ahead, her hands splayed over the magazine. He let himself drop heavily into his armchair.

"The point is to know whether he is totally wrong," she went on. "Here, for instance, where he says. . . ," she tried to find the place with her finger. "Never mind, no need to get bogged down in details. Anyway, he is wrong, isn't he?"

The professor did not answer.

"I mean, you stand behind what you wrote. You have to be sure before you reply."

"But I don't intend to reply."

She looked at him, dumbfounded.

"Are you being serious?"

"Absolutely," the professor answered without looking at her. "In fact, if up till this moment I still had a few doubts, now I have none."

With slight apprehension, she asked him:

"Why?"

The professor shrugged his shoulders.

"Because."

"Are you angry at me?"

"No."

"You don't like people to question what you have written. But you know how I am."

The professor bowed his head.

"Yes, I know."

Walking in the sun along Via Meravigli, through the crowd that clustered around the streetlights or zigzagged in between cars, Salutati felt deeply serene. He entered the first bar he came across, the *Lucky Bar,* and ordered a cappuccino and a brioche. Then he walked toward the phone booth at the back, consulted the tiny address-book he had pulled out of his pocket, entered the booth and, as the light automatically went on, dialed a number.

Sitting at a desk in the attic connected to his apartment by a spiral staircase, with bookshelves lining the wall behind him and the ceiling slanting down to a small window looking out on the roofs, Vicini cogitated while the wind rattled the panes and caused the dust to swirl in the light. His eyes roamed among TV antennas and lightning rods, but his mind was focused on a very precise point of his translation: *sol oritur.* The sun rises. The sun dawns. The sun surges. The sun emerges. These are the real difficulties of translation, always hiding behind the most banal, familiar expressions. Unable to control his distress, Vicini got down from his stool and started pacing the room. Finally, he walked to the window, put his face against the dusty panes and looked down. A microscopic crowd was moving between the leaning walls of the buildings. His eyes scanned the façade of the house opposite his, going upwards past the balcony and the shining dome of the *Immacolata,* all the way up to the sun. "Soars," he thought. He had never used that verb to translate *sol oritur.* He went back to his desk and tried writing it down. It did not work. No wonder he had never used it before. And what about the sun breaks through? At that very moment he heard the phone ring downstairs in his apartment. Unsure whether to answer or keep thinking about the sun, he hesitated until, at the third ring, he rushed to the metal trap door, lifted it, ran down the spiral staircase and into the hallway, and picked up the phone.

"Who is it?"

"I know you are meditating in your hermitage," Salutati said. "Will you forgive my intruding?"

"Ah, how are you?"

"But you're out of breath. Would you have rushed to answer had you known it was only me calling?"

"I don't know," Vicini said, sitting down.

"How I love this sort of answer. Linguistic precision is something one learns to appreciate more and more as one grows older."

"Why did you call?"

"You are always in such a hurry," Salutati said, opening and closing the door to turn the light back on in the booth. "What are you working on?"

"A new commentary on *De bello Gallico.*"

"Who is publishing it?"

"CISE."

"They don't pay much," Salutati said. "And knowing you, you might have been wasting a great deal of your time on just one petty point."

"As a matter of fact, I have: *sol oritur.*"

"The sun rises," Salutati said, putting his face close to the glass panels of the booth. "In fact, here in the bar it is already very warm."

"No, I've already rejected 'rises.'"

"I thought as much. I know how fussy you are when it comes to translating, and fully sympathize."

"Are you trying to be ironic?"

"Not a bit, my dear, never with you. To each his own, as the Romans used to say, and they knew what was theirs. But, speaking of the Ancients, have you read the attack on our friend?"

"Yes."

"And what did you think of it?"

"I found it excessive. Hold on a second," with his free hand he poured a little aperitif in one of the glasses on top of the bar trolley. "As I was saying, I found it justified but excessive."

"But you found it justified."

"Absolutely. No doubt about it. Even his best friends wouldn't be able to deny that."

"You're right," Salutati concurred, with gravity, and raised his head. "At least as far as the philological side goes."

"Or the human side, for that matter."

"You're right," Salutati repeated in the same tone of voice. "But tell me, do you have any idea, the slightest inkling, as to who wrote it?"

"Yes, I do, but I could be wrong."

"Who?"

"Daverio."

"The Second-rater?"

"Exactly."

"But why would he do it?"

"There are at least two good reasons," he took the glass from the top of the trolley. "First of all, his wife."

"Daverio's?"

"Of course not, the other's. Didn't you know she was the student of both? Their favorite pupil?"

"No, I did not know that," Salutati answered with a glint in his eyes.

"She never missed one of Daverio's reckless lectures. She was always there, in the first row, listening to him with rapt attention."

"I can well imagine what that meant to Daverio's vanity."

"Of course, she was a real beauty." Vicini paused. "As a matter of fact, still is. And Daverio is only ten years older, not twenty, like the other one."

"But she chose the other."

"She did. But he still can't accept it. If you think of it, Daverio's still very much an adolescent."

"True," Salutati agreed, with some surprise. "Who would have ever thought you could be so perceptive."

"Daverio will never forgive him for it," Vicini continued, unperturbed. "And this would be the first and foremost reason."

"And the second reason?"

"The second reason is that Daverio is unhappy and aggressive. He always puts the best of himself into arguments where he has everything to lose."

"Do you think you could find out whether he is really the one?"

"Sure," Vicini answered, getting up. "Besides, I'm

going to see his rival at the chess club. Anything else you want to know?"

"No," Salutati answered, opening the door of the booth. "That's all for now."

And then he added:

"My best wishes for your Gallic campaign," and hung up.

# III

Whoever, on that bright and fresh April evening, had chanced to turn from Corso Buenos Aires into Viale Tunisia, toward the sun setting behind the highrises in a flight of pigeons and pink clouds, would not have necessarily noticed the young man, with no distinguishing marks, who, with upturned face, had, in passing, examined the numbers above two adjacent doors and had finally entered a third one. If, instead, by a yet less plausible coincidence, our idle spectator had not only spotted the young man, but had also decided to tail him, he would have followed him up a dark staircase to the second floor, where he would have seen him ring a doorbell bearing the name *Santoro Maria.* At which point he couldn't have gotten any closer without attracting attention. He would have had to choose between two options: either to walk up another flight—but for what reason?—or to feign disorientation and, after a short hesitation, take the stairs back down to the street. In either case, he would have missed forever the following dialogue between two people who stood on either side of a closed door.

"Who is it?"

"Excuse me, madam. I know these are not your office hours, but could you please let me in anyway?"

Then, putting his mouth right up against the wooden door:

"It is a very special situation, madam."

"They all are, for that matter."

"But I talked to you this afternoon, please."

The door opened. A tall, big woman, her copious drooping breasts draped by the black dress that stretched over her bulging belly, stood between him and the light of the hallway. The young man nodded and, raising his index finger, asked:

"May I come in?"

"Please, do," the woman answered, moving to the side, but still holding the doorhandle.

The young man walked to the center of a hallway bathed in a greenish light.

"Let's go to my study; don't mind the mess."

Steeped in a musty smell, the room was only lit by the dim light of a bronze lamp, resting on a desk littered with papers. On the floor, the two metal drawers of a file cabinet blocked the way.

"There," the woman gestured toward an armchair with a gray cover. She sat at her desk, and rested her elbows on its top.

"What kind of apartment were you looking for?"

"I would like one without a doorman."   ·

"One room with kitchen and bathroom, right?"

"Yes."

The woman pulled out all sorts of folders and index cards and started sorting them out:

"They are the ones most in demand, as you may well imagine, but there are still a few left."

Suddenly, she stopped shuffling through her papers.

"When do you need it?"

"Well, madam. . . I don't really know."

"But then," she exclaimed, looking him straight in the eyes, "why are we wasting our time?"

"You see, the decision isn't up to me alone."

"But haven't you told her about it?"

"Told whom?"

"Look here," the woman paused. "Don't you want to use this apartment as a pied-à-terre?"

The young man adjusted his glasses.

"I've been renting apartments for thirty years," she continued. "It's obvious you want an apartment for a particular reason. Isn't that so?"

"Yes."

"So!" the woman exclaimed, leaning back in her chair. "Why do you hesitate?"

"Because, you see, madam, I think I might need it, but I am not sure yet. I've come to see you so as to have an idea. . . "

"I know this is none of my business," the woman closed her eyes for a moment, "but are you already intimately involved with this person?"

"Not yet," the young man rested his hands on his knees. "But I'm sure it should happen."

"Is she married?"

"To a professor."

"Why don't you go to a hotel?'

"She'd never do that. That's clear from something she said."

"Oh, we say so many things," the woman was looking at him. "But in the end we always settle for what we get."

Then she added:

"How long has it been going on?"

"A while."

"But then you might need it all of a sudden."

"Yes."

"Have you thought about renting one by the hour? Something that looks like home, with records, a TV, etc., but you only occupy it when you need it. You let me know a little ahead of time, and I'll get you the keys."

"But, is it safe?"

"Absolutely," the woman answered raising her hand. "No doorman, a double set of keys."

"Where?"

"Wherever you want it. Just a second."

And, getting up, she added:

"Let me see."

She pulled the first drawer out of the metal cabinet, put it down on her desk, and started looking through its contents.

"Here we go," she said. "This one is located in Piazza Aspromonte. Fourth floor, elevator. You must call this number and say that I gave it to you. Can you write it down?"

The young man searched his breast-pocket for a pen but couldn't find it.

"Here, take this," she tore a page out of her appointment book. "The number is 276 892."

While the young man, still frantically searching the pockets of his jacket, was finally getting a hold of his pen, she went on:

"There is another one in Via Ampère, top floor, with dormers, wall-to-wall carpeting, and paintings. Are you writing this down?"

The young man, who had finally been able to write down the first number, answered:

"Yes."

"The number for this one is 514 467. In the meantime, you can pay me the fee."

"For two numbers?"

"You give me the money, and I'll give you more numbers." She pulled another index card out of the same file: "This is a studio in Via Canaletto, second floor, 222 625. So?"

Having pulled out his wallet from the inside pocket of his jacket, the young man was now holding the money in his right hand, still hesitating. With a sudden swoop of her arm, the woman snatched it up and tucked it away into a drawer.

"Here is another one, gorgeous, in Via Cardinal Bellarmino, with garden, patio, Venetian blinds. Call 334 759."

She waited for the young man to write everything down and then went on:

"But the best one is in a townhouse in Via Benedetto Marcello. Residential area, quiet, lots of trees, two little apartments, one on the first floor and the other one on the second. There is even a little garden, with plants and gravel. Write this down: 274 638."

"Wait, there is something else," she was rummaging through the drawer when she suddenly stopped:

"No, this is enough. If you want more numbers you'll have to pay me another fee."

"No, thank you," the young man answered, still writing. "This is enough for now."

He raised his head:

"But I promise I'll come back to see you, if I need to," he paused. "And I really hope I will."

The woman pulled her hands out of the drawer:

"Fine."

She watched him fold the paper in four and put it into his breast-pocket, and then told him:

"I hope I'll see you again soon."

She stood up and, walking toward him, around the side of the desk, added:

"The best of luck."

"Thank you," the young man answered, heading toward the door.

"Don't you worry," she told him in the hallway. "These things generally work out in the end."

"Who knows," the young man tarried. "Maybe this is different."

"Of course," she said, unbolting the door. "But maybe not as much as you think." And, giving him a slight push with her left hand, she held out her right one to him and said:

"So long," and, as he turned toward her, on the landing, she slowly closed the door.

The epidiascope is an instrument that projects the images of opaque and transparent objects onto a screen. It is used to enlarge drawings and slides. The professor generally used it to project the codes that he wanted to decipher onto a white screen hooked to the key of one of his taller glassed-in bookcases, but that afternoon he used it to enlarge parts of the letter.

"What sort of clue do you expect to find in a sentence?" his wife had asked him from the door.

Then, she had added:

"You know, you are a real maniac."

"I know," he had answered without turning.

The first sentence that appeared on the bright screen in the darkened study was: "Is it possible to commit a more unbelievable howler?" Staring at it, the professor sat down at his desk. There was something frivolous and inane about the question "Is it possible?" It sounded like the beginning of the querulous letters people sent to newspapers. "Is it possible. . . ." He had always despised people who got angry by mail. He could understand it if they actually did something, but what was the point of wondering whether the world was right the way it was. Even the adjective "unbelievable" was somewhat excessive. That sort of adjective could only work in advertising. Or in the mouth of young people. When he was young, he too found everything "unbelievable." Until then he had believed in a world that did not exist, and so he found the real one hard to believe. But in fact, it was the other one that was unbelievable. That the writer was young was confirmed by the adverb "more" coming before "unbelievable" as if to establish a gradation in disbelief. On the other hand, this linguistic innocence that fell so short of any wonderment had managed to come up with as ferocious a coupling as "howler" and "unbelievable." Who could have chosen such a tone? And, in particular, the word "howler." He reread the entire sentence: "Is it possible to commit a more unbelievable howler?" The tone had suddenly changed. The utterer was no longer angry, now he sounded baffled. His eyes looked calm, his mouth hinted a smile: "Is it possible to commit a more unbelievable howler?" The professor turned a knob to make the sentence appear yet larger on the screen. Swelling, the letters started spilling over the original margins of the line. The tone grew impatient, almost threatening:

"IS IT POSSIBLE TO COMMIT A MORE UNBELIEVABLE HOWLER?"

He turned off the epidiascope and went to the

kitchen. Staring at the white tiles directly in front of his eyes, he swallowed a whole glass of water. Then he returned to his study, switched the epidiascope back on, and isolated another sentence: "As a matter of fact, we are probably surprising him right now." What could the use of the first person plural mean? At the university, it was used by almost all the professors, whereas "I" was left to the students who bounced it about among themselves every time they opened their mouth ("I think that"), with the result that nobody ever paid any attention to what they said. The assistants would automatically shift to "we" the moment they stood in front of a class. He had talked about it to Vicini—there was another possible suspect—one evening while they were playing chess at the chess club. He was losing, and, to distract his opponent, he had suddenly asked him:

"Don't you find it pretentious to use 'we' instead of 'I'?

"Not a bit. Quite the contrary," Vicini had answered keeping his eyes on the chessboard while stroking his beard. "I take it as a sign of modesty."

He had let the discussion drop there.

"From now on, whenever I happen to use it I'll think of you," Vicini had added. Chances were that, had he written the letter, he would have avoided all risk of being recognized, and this was enough to exonerate him.

He opened the window and pushed the shutters back along their tracks. Waves of hot air wafted up from the gravel. The sun was setting. He saw his wife walk down the garden path and push the buzzer to open the gate. Turning back, she saw him at the window and smiled at him. She was wearing a white hat that she protected with her hand as she bent to get into the cab. He barely heard the car take off. Where was she going? It was not her habit to go out at that hour, and particularly not dressed like that. A vast silence hovered over the fields. When he directed his eyes back to the road, the car had disappeared.

He returned to the instrument, but the letters appeared all faded. He pulled the shutters, closed the window, and the room grew dark again. He moved the page too quickly in front of the epidiascope, and all the lines started overlapping, so he made it slide very slowly in front of the lens all the way down to "to eliminate any doubt from the outset." Why "eliminate"? He could have used something more colloquial such as "to nip in the bud," but that verb would have only indicated an action, without all its consequences, whereas "to eliminate" (to remove from the threshold, the *limen*), swept everything away. He remembered the gynecologist's light-blue eyes, in the bright hallway, by the window, when he flatly told him: "We are going to eliminate it." And he had looked at him with hesitation, unable to answer, yet feeling that he would never forget that moment. Even "doubt" was not a casual word. It referred back to its opposite, "certainty," and suggested a need for evidence, a scientific direction. Liverani! How could he have forgotten him. "I should have been in science, not in literature," Liverani had confided to him in a bookstore, one evening, many years ago. "Why, you think you are doing literature?" he had answered. In the meantime Liverani had pulled a book by Weyl, *Symmetry*, off the paperback's shelf, and, leafing through it, had shown him a few pictures: flowers, crystals, honeycombs, a fountain in a Moorish courtyard. With his finger, he had drawn his attention to a note at the bottom of the page that cited a book published in

Berlin in 1932, *The Problem of Right and Left in the Human and Animal World,* and had said:

"These are the issues that fascinate me."

He also remembered that on another occasion, in the library, as they were standing by an open window overlooking the gardens, waiting for the attendant to bring them their books, Liverani had asked him, with a smile:

"Are you still into etymologies?"

And then he had told him of his theory concerning the Mirmidons, the people who had followed Achilles to the siege of Troy, and of how their name came from *myrmekes,* ants, and of how Helen could be seen as the queen of the termitarium, as the heart that kept it alive for as long as it went on beating, and that would kill it the moment it stopped. Which was why they had fought for ten solid years. And since he had found this hypothesis quite suggestive, if daring, and had asked him why he was not doing something with it, Liverani had answered:

"Because I'd rather leave you the privilege of making mistakes. I like hypotheses but, as a rule, prefer certainty. To each his limits."

And so, torn between his love for science and his love for ancient history, Liverani had become a strange amphibian and had specialized in ancient science.

The light of the epidiascope, issuing from an opening on top of the instrument, cast the shadow of his hand onto the ceiling. What was the book Liverani had given him a few years ago?

He opened the bookcase behind him and, letting his fingers run along the spines of the books, he stopped at a leather bound, India-paper edition of Helian's treatise on animals. On the title page, Liverani had written in his clear, small hand: "Which one do you identify with? The Arabian Phoenix?" And, on yet another occasion, after listening to him talk about his studies, Liverani had told him:

"So, you believe in immortality!"

It was a winter morning in Via Conservatorio, and the snow had been shovelled and heaped into tall pyramids on the black sidewalks. And since he had not asked him for any explanation, Liverani had continued:

"You don't believe you're going to die. It doesn't even cross your mind."

And then he had added:

"Maybe you've never gone through a real crisis, but there's still time."

The professor's jaw suddenly dropped. He leaned his back against the bookcase and let himself slide into the chair. But the letter said: "There is always time," and not "there is still time." His mouth closed, blood flowed to his face. Liverani would not have used the adverb "always." "It is a word that belongs to a different world," he had been saying since their university days. "What do we know about always?" He was much too careful, much too meticulous in his use of language to employ a word he did not believe in. When he talked, he would often correct himself, and when he was finished he would at times go back and modify something he had said at the beginning. Writing was very hard work for him. "I am a lake that has to be squeezed out of a dropper," he had told him one day, as they were sitting in the park in front of the planetarium dome.

He said out loud:

"There is always time."

And then:

"There is still time."

The effect was the same.

Then, he lowered his voice and said:

"There is always time."

He looked at the darkness around him and, with a low, deep voice, said:

"There is always time."

No, it could not be Liverani.

He pushed the button at his right and, raising his face toward the bright chandelier, closed his eyes. Then, he pulled *The Voice of Antiquity* out of the epidiascope and folded it. He was walking toward the door when he suddenly realized that in fact he had just read: "there is still time." He wavered, leaned on the desk with the palms of his hands, opened the journal and, without searching for it, immediately saw the sentence. It was Liverani.

As his heartbeat kept getting faster, he lay on the sofa at the back of the study and turned on his side. Then he put a pillow under his head and with his thumb tried to find his pulse. It had never been so rapid. He looked at the glowing face of his watch and counted twenty beats in ten seconds. A hundred and twenty a minute. He remembered the diaphanous face of the cardiologist: "Try to avoid strong emotions." His temples were also throbbing. His left arm was tingling. Suddenly, he was afraid he was going to die. He shut his eyes. His belly, resting on the sofa, heaved at every breath. He thought he should think of nothing. Muffled street noises reached his ears. By and by, the tingling subsided, the blood flowed more slowly through his veins, his breathing grew quieter. He could hardly hear it. He reopened his eyes and saw his books behind the glass.

# IV

Liverani lived on one of the top floors of a highrise whose upper portion spread out like the cap of a mushroom. A bachelor, prematurely retired thanks to a special law that favored ex-military personnel, he had spent all his savings on the down payment for that immense apartment, which he no longer had any money to furnish, let alone to finish paying for. It had been a great deal, he still maintained, but of such vast proportions that it had completely ruined him. To repay the thirty-year mortgage he had taken out, he had been forced to fall deeper into debt and to increase the editorial work that he had always thought he would give up as soon as he had retired. Tired and distressed, he would roam through the bare rooms where paintings hung as if in a museum. A six-shelf glass case contained fossils, shells, rocks, flintstones, lichens. In front of each piece a tag indicated the exact date and place of the find. There were times, in winter, when it was impossible to see a thing out of the circular windows in the hallway; the fog below was so dense that the building emerged out of it like a beacon above a sea of clouds.

That afternoon, Liverani had fallen asleep while reading an essay by Max Jammer on the concept of strength in antiquity. He had woken up once, hardly an hour later, feeling so weak and drowsy that he had again shut his eyes and had let himself sink back into a beneficial torpor out of which he had resurfaced only one hour and a half later. He had felt a strange languor spread through his body, passing under his forehead and cleansing it, seeping into his legs and feet, causing him to shiver with pleasure. He had walked to the mirror to check his face. Just a little sleep was enough to transform it and reabsorb the bags under his eyes. That afternoon, his wrinkles had practically disappeared, his skin, toning up, had erased them. He had shuffled through the hallway, with limp arms and lowered eyelids, and had gone to the kitchen to make a cup of coffee. Then, venturing into the servants' bathroom, the only one he ever used, he had washed his face alternately with warm and cold water, as had been his habit for the last thirty years to keep his complexion fresh. Finally, he had returned to the study and, feeling full of energy and in top form to work, had instead reclined in an armchair and had again closed his eyes. True, he had immediately clutched the armrests as if to give himself a push to get up. But, in fact, he had remained in his place, without moving, while the sun kept declining in the circular windows of the hallway.

Only when dusk had fallen on the room, did he get up from the chair and, raising his right hand and addressing a vague smile to an imaginary audience, solemnly said:

"The theme of this lecture is potentially immense...."

"No."

He bowed his head.

"Once again."

He pursed his lips and gazed straight ahead:

"The subject I shall address myself to this evening, in front of this select audience. . . ."

He paused.

"The subject of my lecture, this evening," he started again, "is both suggestive and extremely vast."

He looked around and said:

"It concerns Aristotle's lost works."

He closed his eyes for a second.

"Allow me, please, a brief parenthesis."

Who in the world could have forbidden it?

"First of all, a brief parenthesis. Bardon has written a wonderful book: *Unknown Latin Literature*."

He shook his head.

"No."

"Just a brief digression."

He walked to his desk, rested his palms on top of it and, staring at the print of Rembrandt's *Susan at Her Bath*, on the white wall, he said:

"I would like to ask you a very simple question. What remains of the literature of antiquity?"

He let a few seconds go by and then said:

"A minute portion. Yes, ladies and gentlemen, a minute portion that includes invaluable treasures, but that is nevertheless tiny as opposed to what has disappeared."

He glanced at the door that led into the hallway and went on:

"In other words, the bulk of ancient literature has been forever lost, even though we are aware of its existence. There is a wonderful book, by Bardon, titled

49

*Unknown Latin Literature.* Well, ladies and gentlemen, if we considered this question in terms of space, much more space. . . ."

He gave a start.

"Twice as much space."

He stared at the circular windows, then half-closed his eyes and continued:

"Yes, ladies and gentlemen, a minute portion. Bardon has written a wonderful book, *Unknown Latin Literature.* A simple list of the works that have been lost, whether destroyed by fire or invasions. . . ."

He lowered his voice and said:

"Forget fire and invasions. . . ."

He tried to gather his thoughts, his chin resting on his chest, then he lifted his face:

"How many works have survived the shipwreck of antiquity?"

He popped his eyes.

"Very few."

He nodded.

"Yes, ladies and gentlemen, virtually nothing."

His eyes strayed toward the white wall.

"The literature we have lost is like an ocean on which few survivors float."

He passed his hand over his forehead.

"What am I saying?!"

He remained silent. He could hear himself breathe, no doubt because of the adenoids.

"This is why unknown literature so intrigues our scholars."

"That's better," he muttered.

"For centuries, scholars have devoted their lives to it, relying on what the surviving texts say, and at times even on what they do not say."

He essayed a captivating smile.

"I wouldn't want to sound paradoxical."

He made a sweeping gesture in the air as if to erase a blackboard.

"And here you might well wonder," he went on. "Rather," and he leaned on the desk with the palms of his hands. "At this point you might well ask me...."

He stopped and then started again, enunciating his words more slowly and clearly:

"At this point you might well ask me how one can reconstruct nonexistent texts."

"Rather, lost texts."

He pursed his lips.

"By relying on what the other texts say. And, at times..."

He hesitated.

"On what they do not say."

He bowed his head, and then, with renewed vigor, went on:

"That's right, ladies and gentlemen. Reticence and silence often speak louder than words. *Argumentum ex silentio*. But there is another extraordinary aspect to this question."

He took a long breath.

"There is often more to say about what is not than about what is."

He went to the window in the hallway and looked down. The city was being swallowed by darkness. He turned his back to the window and, leaning his shoulders against it, said:

"This is, to a certain extent, the case of the lost works of Aristotle."

Head bowed and hands clasped behind his back, he strode down the full length of the hallway.

"Hmmm."

51

He squinted, as if to see further, and went on:

"What was left of Aristotle? The notes written for his pupils and by his pupils and. . ." and here his voice was drowned by the long, loud ring of the door-bell right behind him.

He wheeled around at once and looked through the peephole, even though, due to a stupid oversight, the lens had been installed in the wrong direction. The visitor's face appeared grotesquely distorted, with tiny eyes and forehead and a gargantuan mouth. Liverani placed his palms on each side of the peephole and positioned his eye as close as possible to the lens: immediately the mouth puckered up and the eyes popped out. Suddenly the face got nearer and a gigantic pupil filled the peephole. Liverani jumped back. Then, tucking a corner of his shirt inside his pants, he tiptoed back to the door. As he was readjusting his eye to the lens, the bell rang again, right by his ears. He waited for the sound to subside and then looked, but this time saw nothing. Maybe his visitor was leaning against the door, thus covering the peephole. Maybe he had also placed the palms of his hands against the wood and was now eavesdropping. Straightening up as quietly as he possibly could, Liverani inadvertently bumped against the brass umbrella-stand that stood by the door. He turned in time to see it totter briefly before decidedly tilting in the opposite direction: he managed to get a hold of it one second before it went crashing onto the floor, but still too late to prevent one of its handles from swinging against the polished tiles. Then he stood still, holding his breath.

"Are you going to let me in or not?"

"Ah, it's you!?"

He stood up and put the umbrella-stand back in its

place. Then he unlatched the door and opened his arms.

"Would you believe I did not recognize you?!"

Having descended twenty-five floors in an elevator, and having safely emerged into the balmy evening in the little square at the foot of the highrise, the professor felt a sudden burst of energy spread through his legs. With a spring in his step, he crossed the street and dove into the yellow glow of an alehouse. There were only two patrons, both sitting on stools in the wood-panelled room. He ordered a medium-sized, dark beer and watched the barman remove the head from the rim of the glass with a wooden spatula. He drank it down in a single draft. Back in the little square, he patted the pocket of his jacket with the tips of his fingers and felt the outline of the book Liverani had just given him. He walked toward the light of a lampost, pulled the book out, and started to gently leaf through it. It was a short essay on Chimera. "Don't expect it to be thorough," Liverani had told him, handing him the book. "I'm tired of rigor. I've always sacrificed my best ideas to it. Don't you find it a touch too cadaverous? *Rigor mortis.*" Pretending he had not understood, he had asked him: "In what sense?" and Liverani had smiled: "You should ask!" Then he had continued: "Do you remember all the books I wanted to write? Which ones did I finally write? Only the safest ones. And at every book I lost more ground. But I am realizing it only now. And you," he had let his hand drop onto the armrest. "What have you done with all your ideas about the origins of speech? You gave a little speech about the idea of origin, wrote a few preliminary essays, said a word or two concerning the scope of the question, the perspectives to take, and so on and so forth." He had run his hand through his hair. "I am reading Tolstoy's journals," he had added. "He did not believe in preliminary work. He kept saying: 'If I'm still alive tomorrow,' and so he went on living." "Maybe Tolstoy believed in something," he had answered. "And you, what do you believe in?" Liverani had asked him.

How could he have possibly suspected him? When he had pulled *The Voice of Antiquity* out of his briefcase and had placed it, already opened at page 82, right under his nose, Liverani's quick eyes had glanced at him with astonishment.

"A libel against you?"

And once he had started reading, his pupils had followed the flow of every line without skipping a single one. Once finished, he had kept his head bowed over the page. Then, knitting his brow, he had said:

"This is clearly an expression of personal hatred."

"Wouldn't you say so?"

"Yes, definitely."

"Who do you think did it?"

"Hmm."

He had insisted.

"At least tell me the first name that comes to your mind."

"Why, what difference would it make?"

"Maybe none. I just wanted to know whether we are thinking the same thing."

Then Liverani had said, somewhat tentatively: "Daverio?" and he had felt as if someone had suddenly pushed him over the edge and he were gasping for air, the way he had, as a boy, when someone had shoved him off the diving board.

"Please, don't get me wrong," Liverani had quickly

added. At which point, following an unexpected and irresistible impulse, he had asked, without even knowing why:

"Because of my wife?"

"Yes, I think so."

"You are out of your mind. My wife has nothing to do with all this."

Liverani looked surprised.

"You are the one who brought it up. Besides, knowing Daverio's previous history. . ."

"What previous history?"

"He was courting her before you did. You were aware of it, weren't you?"

"No, I wasn't."

Liverani had opened his arms in dismay.

"I am sorry. It's common knowledge on campus. I guess it is really true that the last person to learn of certain things is the one who is most directly involved."

"Which things?" he had answered, trying to keep calm.

"No, it's not what you think. I don't believe that for a second. Still, I think Daverio has something against you. I really do. And that letter is very personal."

He had sat up in his chair and had continued:

"In other words, he could have written it. Because it was certainly written by someone who knows you well. Take me, for instance," he had added, looking at him. "I could have certainly written it."

"I know."

"Maybe you even suspected me."

"No, of course not. Otherwise I wouldn't be here."

Going up the steps of his house, hat in hand, eyes turned toward the illuminated window, the professor leaned against the stone balustrade and thought:

"What am I doing?"

At that very moment the light in the living room went off and the one in the hallway went on. When the front door opened, his wife, seeing him only a few feet away, in the dark, gave a start.

"You scared me."

"Are you going out?"

"Yes," she answered uneasily, her restless blue eyes growing gradually firmer. "I thought I had told you."

"Have a minute?"

Hesitating, she glanced at her wristwatch.

"Yes."

She walked back into the hallway.

"Did you see Liverani?"

"Yes. I don't think he is the one."

He walked into the dining room and sat down at the table.

"Is there anything to eat?"

"Yes, I put something out for you in the kitchen."

"Won't you sit down?"

She cast one more glance at her wristwatch and then sat on the edge of the chair.

"Tell me."

"Liverani thinks it's Daverio."

"What?"

"Hold on a second," the professor said, got up, and went to the liquor cabinet at the other end of the room. As he bent down to open it, she asked· him:

"Why Daverio?"

"He may be jealous."

"Of me?"

The professor turned to her with a look of surprise:

"No. What do you have to do with it?"

He was again standing up, glass in hand.

"Professional jealousy," he explained. "You know they call him the Second-rater. You have nothing to do with it."

"Right."

The professor put his glass down onto the table.

"Do you still see him?" he asked her.

"Yes."

She had started pouting, the way he liked her to, even though he knew it was often a prelude to an unpleasant confession.

"Often?"

"Yes. Is there anything wrong with it?"

"It depends," the professor answered sitting down. "You never told me."

"I didn't think it mattered. Besides, you always imagine things."

The professor hesitated:

"So, it did matter somewhat."

"To him, maybe. Not to me."

The professor was silent for a minute.

"Is he after you?"

"No, I don't think so."

Then, on second thought, she added:

"Maybe. We talk."

The professor was observing her.

"There is no point asking you questions," he told her. "You are constantly going on about sincerity, and yet you are the most duplicitous person I know."

"You always want to know what crosses my mind."

The professor shook his head:

"No. Not insofar as I'm concerned. I just don't want you to hide from me what goes on between you and Daverio."

"Nothing," she immediately answered.

Then she added.

"At least, nothing that concerns you."

The professor looked perplexed.

"Rather," she went on, changing the tone of her voice. "Tell me about Liverani. What made you change your mind?"

"I don't know," the professor answered wearily. "Suddenly it all seemed quite absurd. Why would he do something like that?"

"Why don't you ask somebody else?" she insisted. "Vicini, for instance, he is always so well informed."

"True," the professor agreed. "You are right."

"Weren't you supposed to meet him at the Chess Club?"

"Yes, this evening."

He looked at his watch.

Standing up, she asked him:

"May I go now?"

"Of course," the professor answered standing up in his turn. "By the way, where are you going?"

Half an hour later, as he was crossing the hallway, the professor noticed the outline of his belly in the mirror. He turned around and looked at himself. How often, as a young man, returning home half drunk after a night of bar-hopping with his friends, had he looked at himself long and hard in that same mirror so that later he might be able to remember his face. And yet, now, he could not remember it. His body seemed to have shrunk and spread out. He removed his glasses, but when he looked at himself again his eyes seemed absent.

He walked into the living room and phoned for a cab. He waited for it by the open window. The fields, in the evening, were all abuzz. He stood motionless, listening. Then, he closed the shutters, locked the front door and, in a few steps, was at the gate. The cab had already pulled up. As he was getting in, the driver turned his head:

"Where to?"

The professor sat back on the black leather. His eyes shone in the dark.

"Via Ariosto, please. The Paul Morphy Club."

# V

When Paul Morphy sailed for Europe, in 1958, he
had already beaten the best chess players in his
country. He had learned to play when he was eight,
and had soon defeated his teacher, who also happened
to be his father. Then he had beaten his older brother,
his uncle, and his grandfather, in that order. Then he
beat Eugène Rousseau, casually traveling through
New Orleans, and, after him, the Hungarian
Löwenthal. In 1957, he had gone on to beat all the
masters competing in the International Tournament
in New York. At which point, he had challenged every
American player, giving them the advantage of the
first move and one pawn. Nobody had accepted,
except for Stanley who, after being defeated four times
in a row, had given up. Then the New Orleans Chess
Club had invited the English champion, Staunton,
offering to pay for the trip and all related expenses,
but he had refused to go. It was precisely in order to
play with him that, in 1958, Morphy had sailed for

Europe, but, once he got to London, Staunton refused to meet him. Morphy beat other opponents, among whom Owen, Bird, Harrwitz, Anderssen, and Montgrédien, but not Staunton who, in the meantime, was defaming him to the press. Morphy went back to London to meet with him, but Staunton told him he had more important things to do. When Morphy returned to the United States he had yet to play with him. He died a few years later and Staunton managed never to lose a single game to him.

The club bearing his name had been founded thirty years earlier by a count whose sole official occupation in life had been chess. A blown-up photo that hung at the top of the stairway showed him tall, thin, perfectly bald, with a freckly pate and crinkly face, pensively sitting in front of an ivory chessboard. On the tapestry to its right, a naked Daphne was grappling with Apollo on a background of gold leaves. A passage, at the far end of the balcony, led to the chess library bequeathed by the count to the club and containing six thousand volumes, bound in red leather with solid gold inscriptions. It was believed he had only read a few, but he had leafed through the others and had fondly stroked each volume before placing them behind glass in his library. As a player he had been melancholic and modest. He had toured the world, from one tournament to the next, awarding cups and medals and playing friendly games with grandmasters who, out of respect, gave him no initial advantage and regularly beat him by a narrow margin. His interest in the game was mostly theoretical and ultimately superficial, as if, even in this case, he had not dared venture too far. As he himself admitted, his was an imaginary interest, based on the intense pleasure he felt whenever he looked at the diagram of a game, at the symbolic transcription of each move and at the meticulous analytical comments that accompanied them and which he did not read but rather glanced at with the same satisfaction his ancestors must have felt while riding through their own lands in a surrey. Speaking of him, the current president of the club, who had known him when he was still a boy, used to say that ultimately, in his eyes, he had always been a count and that just as he was born a count, he had lived and died as one. By which, he was probably also referring to the detachment with which he had experienced and controlled his passion, until he had ennobled and surmounted it.

During his last years, his technical opinions had earned him a few followers. He used to write short articles which he signed as "Caissa," the nymph of chess, for a magazine he had financed for over thirty-five years and to which he regularly contributed a tiny bibliographical survey. Two years before his death he had made provisions for a bequest: the first and second floor of his palace had gone to the chess club along with a small endowment. Since then, he had stopped playing chess or talking about it. He traveled abroad, in search of the ideal climate. Back in the city, he would take residence in a wing of the guest-quarters and never even attended the traditional receptions in the honor of some grandmaster who happened to be passing through. The president still remembered him, one afternoon in the little gravelly garden, as he sat on a bench, basking in the sun with half-closed eyes. "I have only just begun to live," he had told him. Two months later he was dead and his wax mask had been placed in the first floor lobby, between the oil portrait of his father, in equestrian pose on the cobblestones of a courtyard, and that of his mother, vaporously rosy and very young against the thick verdure of a hedge.

His head held high, the professor crossed the first room between rows of players bent over chessboards at their respective tables, with the tournament clocks set high in the bays of the windows. Looking straight ahead at each successive door, he passed from the second room to the third where his eyes resumed their normal expression as they focused on Vicini who, alone in a corner facing a chessboard, was smoking a cigar and studying the moves of an imaginary game. To his right, on the table, lay an open chess book.

"You know, the better I get the more convinced I am about one thing," Vicini told him, without raising his head, as soon as he became aware of the other's proximity.

"What would that be?" the professor asked as he sat opposite him.

"All things considered, the Sicilian Defense remains the best opening."

He rested his cigar on the ashtray and, with a broad smile that expressed self-satisfaction more than the pleasure of seeing his interlocutor, asked him:

"So, how are you?"

The professor drew his chair closer to the table.

"You look tired," Vicini added.

"Have you read the last *Voice of Antiquity?*"

"Yes. I have even seen the letter concerning you."

"What do you think of it?"

Vicini, putting the cigar back into his mouth and tilting his head to the side, did not answer. Then, swathed in smoke, he started placing the chess pieces on the board. After which, he slowly said:

"I think you have an enemy."

"That's all? Who could it be?"

Vicini nodded.

"I've got to think about it."

Convinced that knowledge meant caution and that caution meant torpor, whenever Vicini was supposed to think, he closed his eyes and, first of all, stopped thinking altogether. Portly, with a flabby face and sagging cheeks, in time he had physically turned into the antithesis of his father, a regular officer and occasional poet, who had oppressed him throughout his adolescence and had made him wish he would grow up as soon as possible: how often had he blushed with shame and grief at the banging of fists on a table and at the pathos of heart-felt declamations. He had reacted by letting his beard grow and by assuming a severe mien and a solemn tone of voice. Already then, one of his favorite expressions was: "This question is not nearly as simple as it may, at first, appear." And he was also wont to say: "It is not wise to get out at the first stop," even though that was precisely where he used to get out, never daring to go any further. He had always looked forward to growing old, to becoming the opposite of his father, and, by and by, he had almost succeeded. By increasingly limiting his ambitions and turning abnegation into an ideal he had ended up marrying a woman who had agreed to marry him for exactly the same reasons. His academic specialty was interlinear translation, the very subject he had shunned as the emblem of laziness when, back in high school, he was a whiz at Latin. Having finally found true serenity at fifty, he had been rudely surprised and left in a state of painful stupor by the so-called "student revolution." But he had gradually recovered, and his newly conquered wisdom had smoothed the lines in his face and brought back sleep, while lending a quieter timbre to his voice and a rare but luminous hint of melancholy to his eyes.

"So, essentially you're asking me for an opinion, is that so?" Vicini said, raising both eyelids and eyes. "In short, you want me to give you a name. And so I will."

The professor leaned over the table. Vicini went on:

"First of all, I don't think this is the letter of a, what shall I say, help me. . ."

Waiting for the right word, he lapsed back into deep meditation.

"An imbecile," the professor suggested.

"Imbecile! You must be kidding me. This is someone who knows exactly what he's up to, and you know that for a fact. What I meant is that there is more to this than mere professional animosity. As you must know by now, philologists positively despise each other."

"They are not the only ones."

"True, but they are more acrimonious than anybody else. I have never understood why. Maybe because they are exasperated by the fact that they have to devote so much time to somebody else's work. But, in this particular instance, there is something more."

"Yes, I feel the same way."

"This is somebody who hates you for what you are and knows how to hit you exactly where it hurts the most."

"That is?"

"You are asking me?" Vicini said, putting the last piece onto the board. "And yet there is no simpler answer: your learning."

"Forgive me," he added after looking at him. "I'm telling you this as a friend, you understand. To demonstrate that in order to hurt someone one has to know where to hit. And this person knew exactly where to aim. The fact that you are so upset proves it."

The professor remained silent.

"Yes, he has really upset you. And he has been able to hit you in the right spot not just because he questions your competence but also because of the tone he uses, full of irony and spite. And the tone is everything. Or do you happen to think that what counts most is words? Are you so superstitious as to believe in the power of words?"

"Enough!" the professor exclaimed, his eyes suddenly red around the rim. "All I want from you is a name. I'm much too old to listen to your lectures. That's not what I asked you."

"Don't worry, I am going to give you your name," Vicini answered nonchalantly. "I think it's Daverio."

The professor looked at him, aghast:

"You too?"

"Why? Has someone else come up with his name? Salutati, perhaps?"

"No. Did he talk to you?"

"Of course. Did you really think he wouldn't!"

The professor bowed his head:

"Of course. I should have known."

Vicini moved the king's pawn up two squares and started the game.

"And, I suppose, the reasons why you suspect Daverio have nothing to do with learning. Am I right?" the professor asked.

"Of course. Forget learning, at least in this case."

He relit his cigar and, gesturing toward the board, asked him:

"Aren't you playing?"

# VI

At nine o' clock the following morning, sure of making a mistake, the professor was waiting for Daverio under a plane tree full of birds, near the newspaper stand at the corner of Via Lucano and Via Ennio. Now and then, without turning his head, he cast a sidelong glance toward Piazza Insubria. He had barely opened the paper when, in the shop window opposite him, he saw the reflection of Daverio crossing the street in the direction of the stand. He started to read without understanding a single word. Then, unsure whether he should go on reading until the other, barely two steps away, had recognized him, or whether he should put down his paper and walk toward him with open arms, he lowered the paper and, feigning a sudden change of mind, cast a glance at the sidewalk clock and started walking resolutely toward the appliance store on the opposite sidewalk. Before crossing the street he looked to his right and to his left, at which point his eyes almost met those of

Daverio, who, having just bought a paper, was putting it into his briefcase. He immediately redirected his eyes to a van which was being unloaded in front of a fruit store. He expected the pressure of a hand on his shoulder would keep him from crossing the street, but nobody held him back. He waited one more minute, patting the pockets of his jacket, as if searching for something, then, slowly and absent-mindedly, he started crossing the street and was barely missed by a bicyclist who, in full swerve, shouted at him:

"Idiot!"

Disconcerted, the professor jumped back onto the sidewalk in time to see, on his right, the bicyclist pedal away in a wake of muttered insults, and, on his left, Daverio making his way past the tables of an outdoor café. He suspected Daverio had pretended not to see him, just as he had, and felt that he had unwittingly given him yet another advantage and that Daverio, walking away, was growing larger and larger whereas he, still standing under his plane tree, was getting smaller and smaller. Absurdly, he hoped that Daverio would turn and wave to him. But when, at the second intersection, Daverio turned the corner, his doubts became intolerable and, without hesitating any further, he started following the other's footsteps along Via Lucano.

Gradually quickening his stride, he also reached the second intersection, but when he turned onto Via Farsaglia, Daverio was nowhere to be seen. To his right unfolded the tall wall of Opus Dei, and to his left, on top of the steps where a man was setting up a flower stand, sat a solitary red-brick church.

Daverio had entered it only a few minutes earlier.

"Please, Lord, make her love me back," he prayed while walking along the aisle.

"I know my request is absurd, but, please, Lord, I beseech you, help me anyway."

He had reached the middle of the nave and was looking for the stoup.

"I really shouldn't be asking this of you, of all people."

The stoup stood on his right, by a pillar. He dipped the tips of his fingers into the water and made the sign of the cross. As he walked on toward the altar, drops of holy water kept pearling down his forehead.

"I know you will come to my help," he murmured.

He knelt down in a pew.

"I shall atone for all my sins, Lord, I shall repay all my debts," he went on while staring at the floor. "I will be good."

At these last words, he inadvertently raised his voice and suddenly became aware of an old woman who, further down to his right, was staring at him. He immediately turned his eyes to a red votive lamp, in front of him, and stared at it intently. The image grew increasingly blurred as tears welled in his eyes.

"It's not the happiness that matters," he closed his eyes. "It would change my entire life."

A sexton stopped to kneel before the altar and then proceeded toward a little velvet door.

"It would make me a better man."

He reclosed his eyes and saw a cluster of fiery dots, which, as soon as he looked up again, coincided with the flames of the candelabra on the altar.

"I don't know what is becoming of me, Lord," he went on. "I am going through a very difficult time."

He passed his hand over his forehead and felt it burning.

"I can't wait any longer."

He raised his face and rested his eyes on the golden door of the tabernacle.

"I know I should stop asking you for this," he went on. "Especially since it is something you can't condone."

He panted slightly.

"But you alone can give it to me."

"Tell me whether I'll be able to have it. Whether she will leave him."

"All I want is a sign from you."

He fell silent.

Breathing deeply, he remained perfectly still for a long while, his eyes closed.

Then he stood up and made the sign of the cross.

He started walking toward the exit. In the light that fell from the stained-glass windows, he saw a golden triangle.

He turned back to face the altar.

"Thank you," he said.

At the bottom of the steps, under the red awning of a flower stand, among the hydrangeas, Daverio saw the professor looking in his direction. He quickly walked down to him and held out his hand.

"How are you?"

"Not bad, and you?"

"So, so," Daverio answered with a vague smile. "What brings you here?"

"I was on my way to Valisi, to get a book." Then, tilting his head toward the church, he added. "I didn't know you were a worshiper."

"Worshiper! What a big word!"

"All right. A believer, if you prefer."

"Yes, that's much better," said Daverio, starting to walk toward Viale Umbria.

"I don't seem to remember you were so religious a few years ago."

Daverio shook his head.

"I have always believed, in my own way."

The professor was listening to him attentively, his eyes fixed on the street ahead.

"So, according to you, there are several ways to believe?"

"Yes."

"Give me an example."

"Well," Daverio looked around. "I don't know."

He added:

"I remember the story of a woman who killed herself, told by a Russian author, but I can't remember who, Dostoevsky or Turgenev. . ."

"It doesn't matter," the professor interrupted him. "What did she do?"

"She threw herself out the window with a prayer book in her hands."

"And this is the way you believe?" asked the professor, stealing a look at him.

"Maybe," Daverio answered, hinting at a smile. "Even though you might have some difficulty reconciling faith and suicide."

"Indeed. Does the idea of suicide also attract you?"

"Why not? After all, it is only an anticipation. I believe that diseases, as well as death, only occur when one wants them, when one is tired of being the way one is."

The professor adjusted his glasses on the bridge of his nose.

"I didn't know you had such ideas."

"In fact, I didn't. I started getting them after my fortieth birthday, when I realized I was also involved."

He ran a finger inside his shirt-collar and added:

"Do you know what Trotsky used to say? That old age is the most unforeseeable event in a man's life."

"But that is a paradox! And you take him seriously?"

"To the letter."

The professor stopped walking and turned toward him with an incredulous look.

"You really are strange, you know."

"You too," Daverio answered. "Though you're still unaware of the fact. You belong to the category of the immortals."

The professor smiled.

"I could swear somebody else has already told me that. But I can't remember who."

Trying to remember the name, he stopped walking. Suddenly he hit his forehead with the palm of his hand and said:

"Liverani!"

"Ah," Daverio said, bowing his head. "Too bad."

"Why? Don't you like him?"

"No."

"Has he done something to you?"

"No. Why, do you only detest people who have done something to you?"

"Yes. Why, don't you?"

"No."

"Really! I find this very interesting," the professor said slowing down. "So, why do you dislike him? Because of the way he is?"

"Yes."

"So, the same might also be true for me?"

Daverio turned to look at him:

"What do you mean? What does it have to do with you?"

The professor's voice wavered a little:

"You know about that letter attacking me, don't you? Is that the sort of enemy he is?"

When the professor raised his eyes, Daverio turned his face toward the traffic light.

"I would like to know what motivated him to write it," the professor went on. "That's all I want to know."

He kept looking at Daverio, waiting for him to answer, but he remained silent.

Then, he asked him:

"If you were in my shoes, how would you react?"

"Like you."

He had turned toward him and was looking at him with a mixture of excitement and curiosity.

He added:

"First I'd go through the list of my enemies."

The professor nodded.

"But not only enemies you're aware of," Daverio went on. "Also the ones we were talking about a little earlier. The ones who can't forgive you for being the way you are."

"You mean, the gratuitous ones."

"If that's what you want to call them. They could be mine, yours, everybody's."

"But if I don't know who they are, how can I find them?"

Daverio shrugged his shoulders.

"With the help of your imagination," he said. "By trying to remember everything you know."

"That's what you call imagination?"

"Yes, precisely. We always discover what we already know. You already know who did it."

"You think so."

"Yes.

The professor looked at him, perplexed.

"Hmph," he shook his head. "That's not my style."

"I know. But it's the right way."

Both fell silent. Suddenly, Daverio said:

"Weren't you supposed to go to your book dealer?"

"Yes."

"Then I'll come with you."

"Fine," the professor said, perking up. "He was supposed to order two books for me."

"What a good smell," the professor said, sniffing the air and observing the books crammed on the wooden shelves.

"I apologize, Professor. Yours has still not arrived," said the old owner from the niche where he sat, putting his glasses down on the desk.

"But it has already been a month!"

The owner solemnly nodded:

"You know who is taking care of it? Mariani. He receives all the catalogues from all the most important rare-book dealers."

The professor was listening to him with diffidence. "So?"

"So, if he has not found it nobody else will. You must be patient."

"And what about the *Inscriptiones*, by Degrassi?"

"Same thing, you've got to be patient."

Daverio, who had been leaning against the desk, listening to them, approached the professor:

"Guess what's the only thing that still sticks in my mind out of Degrassi's huge tome after all these years? A sentence engraved on a rock, in Tivoli, that said: 'Take me, I'm yours.'"

Moved by curiosity, the owner interjected:

"How did it go in Latin?"

76

"Oh, it was even better," Daverio paused. "*'Cape me, tua sum.'*"

And then, added:

"She puts the most important thing first, the fact that she belongs to him. First she writes 'tua,' and then 'sum.' Whereas we start with 'I am,' after which anything could follow."

He gestured toward the professor and added:

"This is his specialty."

The professor knit his brow and touched his glasses.

"Right."

Then he turned toward the bookseller:

"Very well, Mr. Valisi. I'll be waiting to hear from you."

"My pleasure, Professor."

"Shall we go?" the professor asked Daverio.

A little farther down the street, they came to the university square, along the newly painted, yellow barracks wall.

"I must leave you now," Daverio said, stopping.

"All right," the professor answered.

He shook his hand:

"Please keep in touch."

Daverio smiled:

"The hidden wisdom of everyday language: 'keep in touch.'"

He added:

"Don't worry, I will keep in touch."

As the professor climbed staircase C, clutching the banister with his right hand and letting it go every two steps to seize it again farther up, the assistant, who was watching him from the second landing, started walking down toward him.

"Good morning, Professor."

"Good morning."

"I saw you talking with Daverio."

"Yes."

"Did he say anything?"

"No," the professor answered, panting a little. "I'm back where I started."

They were approaching the top of the stairs:

"Professor. . ."

"Yes?"

"I've learned something new."

The professor stopped to stare at him, then, still turned toward him, started climbing again.

"What have you learned?"

"I'd rather not tell you here," the assistant answered, looking around.

"Who is it?" the professor asked as soon as they had reached the top of the stairs.

The assistant got closer.

"Maybe, instead of looking up," he said, lowering his voice, "we should look down."

# VII

Petite, wearing bangs, a shoulder bag, and dunga-
rees, the girl emerged from the shadow of the doorway
and, walking in the middle of the alley with a smile
on her face, moved toward the professor who was
strolling along right next to the wall. A few feet away
from him, she stopped, but he went on, looking
straight ahead, barely acknowledging her. Without
turning his head, he whispered:

"I had told you never to wait for me on campus."

"But we are not on campus. We are nearly half a
mile away from it. How can you be so scared?"

"Obviously you are not fully aware of our situation," the professor answered through his teeth. "That
figures since I am the one running the greatest risk."

She stopped smiling.

"Please don't be boring."

They had reached Via Morgagni, not far from the
arched shop windows of the Cattadori cellars.

"And please don't start sulking," the girl said. "What's the matter?"

"Nothing."

"Has something happened?"

"No."

"Is it about the piece on 'hypocrite'?"

"Yes."

He stole a look at her.

"You've seen it," he added.

"Everybody has on campus. So what? You'll put him in his place, won't you?"

The professor was staring at the wrought-iron rooster on the shop sign.

"I haven't made up my mind yet," he muttered. "What are they saying?"

"They can't quite figure out who is right and who is wrong," she cautiously answered. "Still, everybody agrees that the tone is offensive. I guess they are waiting to see what your next move will be."

"Are they on my side at least?"

"Well, I don't know. They are waiting."

"Ah."

"What do you expect them to do?"

"Who, me?"

"Besides, you must realize that this is much more important to you than to them."

The professor lowered his head:

"But, according to you it is quite important."

"Please don't put your ideas in my mouth. I've only said that you are the only one who has something at stake in all this."

"Maybe they are laughing."

"No. At most they are smiling, but that's your fault."

"My fault?"

"Yes, because you take everything much too seriously. It makes attacking you worth one's while."

"Worth one's while, is that what you think?"

"Please, please, don't start turning around everything I say."

The professor removed his glasses and started wiping them with his handkerchief. Then, he said:

"Let's change the subject."

They walked on in silence.

Suddenly, the professor asked:

"What about going you know where?"

"Now?"

"It's the only bit of free time I've got."

The girl hesitated.

"As you please. I just wanted to show you something I've written."

"No problem. You'll show it to me after. In the meantime, how about something to drink? I have to make a phone call."

They walked under the chipped arch of the entrance and toward the cashier's desk. He asked her:

"What would you like to drink?"

"A cup of tea."

"Two cups of tea," he told the cashier. "And a telephone token."

While the young woman was proceeding to the counter, the professor went down the first steep step that led to the cellar. Right above his head hovered a painted sign representing an eagle with two heads.

"Hello, it's me," he said, letting the token drop into the box. "I won't be home for lunch. I have to attend a faculty meeting."

"Yes, excruciatingly boring."

He moved to the side to let a waiter, who was

coming back from the cellar, pass with his two bottles of wine.

"Tell me," he paused. "Any news?"

"Ah!"

He looked around and, putting his mouth closer to the receiver, lowered his voice:

"Well, this morning I learned something new."

He turned toward the wall.

"Somebody told me it could be a student," he whispered. "Yes, one of the better ones. But I don't think so. On the other hand, why not?"

"Ah."

He edged up the step and leaned his back against the wall.

"Yes," he nodded. "Anyway, better not make a big deal out of it. After all, it is not that important. Don't you agree?"

He again nodded.

"I'd say so."

He edged back down the step.

"All right."

He was observing the young woman at the counter against the light as she was pouring sugar into her cup of tea.

"How is your headache?"

He turned his face back toward the wall.

"I'm sorry to hear that. Maybe some fresh air would help."

He stared at the step.

"Yes. I'll see you tonight."

He picked up his briefcase from the floor and, holding it in his left hand, walked toward the young woman at the counter.

"Finished?" the young woman asked.

She was the first to get out of the cab in Via XX Settembre. She went to the snack bar of a gas station that stood isolated by the side of the street, at the edge of the first suburban fields. The cab took off between two rows of shining poplars. After some three hundred feet, it went down a slope and pulled over in front of a one-story home surrounded by a little garden that separated it from the other houses. The professor got out, paid, took a good look in every direction, and then opened the gate. He walked along a small paved path to the steps that led to a porch and opened the front door onto a cool, dark hallway. Without turning the light on, he went to the bedroom, pulled the blinds half-way up, left the window ajar, and lay down on the bed. A steady buzz reached him from the garden.

As soon as he heard the intercom, he went to the hallway and pushed a button, only to hear her scream: "It doesn't work!"

The professor had barely stepped onto the porch when, seeing a woman with a child peacefully stroll along the sidewalk right behind the girl at the gate, he turned on his heels and went back in. Hidden behind the curtains of the hallway, he pulled up the blinds and waited for the woman to disappear behind a hedge.

Then he went out again, opened the gate, and hurried back in, followed by the girl who, as soon as she was inside, asked him:

"Doesn't your friend ever use this place? It smells so musty!"

Zooming in from the garden through the open window, the hornet flew straight up to the ceiling, tapped it twice, and then started circling the room.

83

"Get rid of it!" the girl screamed. "Kill it!"

Standing on the bed, the professor grabbed a pillow and threw it against the ceiling. A fine dust fell onto the bed, but the hornet kept on circling. Again the professor threw the pillow which, this time, hit the hornet and sent it reeling against the window pane. There, it got trapped in the folds of the curtains and stopped buzzing.

With a long sigh, the professor lay down again.

"Is it all over?" the girl asked.

"Yes."

The girl rested her chin on her knees.

"I've written another poem," she said.

The professor slowly turned away from her and slipped his arm under the pillow.

"Don't you want to see it?"

"Yes," the professor answered, staring at the wall.

"But promise that you won't lose your patience like you did the last time. I couldn't stand it."

The girl slipped out of bed, pulled a manuscript out of her bag, and then slipped back into bed. She started leafing through the pages, then she stopped and turned to him.

"You know, I just thought about something. But I probably shouldn't tell you. This is not the right moment."

"What is it?" the professor asked, lifting his head from the pillow.

"Something you might not like. It has nothing to do with my poem."

The professor propped himself up on his elbows.

The girl went on:

"Maybe I shouldn't tell you."

"Come on."

"It's something Martelli said about you. But I'm afraid. . ."

The professor sat up.

"Tell me what he said."

"He said that attack puts you back in your place.'

"Did he say it to you?"

"No, he said it to Manni and Manni told me."

"And he didn't say anything else?"

"No. But don't you think that's quite enough for someone who claims to be your friend?"

"My friend! Him!" the professor murmured. "I have learned quite a few things since this whole story started."

"Does this mean that you can no longer put any pressure on him?"

"Why should I?"

"For the poetry contest, what else? Have you already forgotten?"

"Ah."

"As of now, I can only count on four people," the girl went on. "Ferrario, Manni, and, possibly, Martelli."

"And who is the fourth?"

"You, of course!" the girl turned all of a sudden. "Don't tell me you're backing out!"

The professor closed his eyes.

"No, of course not. It's just that my head is not altogether here."

"But mine is! In fact, that's precisely why I have brought you the manuscript. I'd like you to have a look at the last poem. Maybe I should take it out."

She handed him the manuscript opened at the right page.

"Will you look at it?"

The professor stretched his arm toward the bedside table and let his hand grope around in search of his glasses. Then he leaned against the bedstead and placed the manuscript on his knees.

"Wait," the girl said anxiously. She pointed at a couple of lines. "The fourth and the fifth are only tentative. Don't linger on those."

"All right."

"Good. Now you can go on. No. Sorry. Wait. Don't tell me, as you always do, that it sounds like this or that. That doesn't interest me. What I want to know is whether I've been able to say what I wanted to say."

"All right."

"I mean. I don't want a critical judgment. But not because I'm afraid of it. What were you going to do?"

"Well, I was going to tell you whether I liked it or not," the professor answered with a frown.

While reading, he stuck out his lower lip. The girl climbed out of bed and went to close the door to the bedroom. Back on the bed, she saw his eyes hesitating on the second stanza. Then he resumed his reading. At the end, he remained pensive, staring at the manuscript in glum silence.

"It does not convince me," he said.

"Why?"

"The only thing that really interests me is 'useless apologue,' one line before the last."

"And what about the rest."

The professor slid back into a horizontal position.

"The rest sounds false," he answered.

"What!?" the girl said, pulling the manuscript out of his hands. "If there is an honest poem this is it!"

"Maybe you shouldn't be so concerned with sincerity," the professor said, clasping his hands under his nape.

"But you are the one who always makes a big deal out of it."

"Yes, but I was wrong. Rather, I was talking of something else. Another sort of sincerity. All you are doing here is lying in good faith."

The girl climbed again out of bed and started getting dressed.

"I don't like your mood today. I knew I shouldn't have brought up Martelli."

The professor did not move.

The girl asked him:

"Do you want to know what I wanted to say in that poem?"

"If you wish," the professor nodded. "But if I were you, I would eliminate it."

# VIII

For the fifth time in the last three months, the professor, his hands clasped behind his back and his neck stretched forward, was staring at the chessboards displayed in a shop window under the arcades. At last he went in and approached an old salesman in a black frock.

"I would like to buy the largest chessboard you have."

"The one at the center of the window?"

"No, fifteen days ago I saw a larger one."

"Impossible. That's as large as they come."

"I'm afraid you are mistaken."

Then, as if seized by sudden apprehension, he asked:

"Could you have sold it?"

"I'm sorry, sir, but I don't know which one you are talking about. How can you be sure it was larger?"

The professor pointed at the window:

"All you have to do is compare it with the leather case."

"Which leather case?"

"The one that's displayed next to it."

"Would you mind showing it to me?" the salesman asked him. He let the professor go ahead and then joined him in front of the window.

"There," the professor said pointing at a spot in the window. "See the leather case to the right of the chessboard? Now it reaches as far as the fourth square whereas then it barely went beyond the middle of the third one."

"Are you sure?"

"Absolutely. This one is almost one square shorter than the other one."

The lights went on under the arcades.

"Is something the matter, sir?" the woman who owned the shop asked him from the door.

"Yes, madam," the professor answered, touching his hat. "Let me explain."

He returned inside the shop, followed by the salesman.

"How can I help you?"

"First of all, I should let you know that this is my fault, madam. I should have bought it as soon as you displayed it in the window, three months ago."

"What are you talking about?" the woman briskly retorted.

"A very large, rosewood chessboard."

"But it is right there."

The professor patiently shook his head.

"No, madam, I am sure it is not."

He hesitated:

"Maybe you sold it?"

"Yes, three days ago."

The professor sighed:

"Well, you see. . ."

"But this one is exactly like it."

"No, madam, even the pieces were different."

The woman cast a knowing glance at her salesman. "Really?"

"Yes. These are also large Stauntons, but they are a little bit smaller than the other ones."

Pressing a finger against her forehead, the woman concentrated a while, then, slowly, pausing in between words, said:

"Yes, sir. Now I remember. You are right. These are number six, but there is also a larger size."

"Yes."

"Which means that you might also be right as far as the chessboard goes."

"Obviously."

"But there is a problem," the woman said, looking at him with doleful eyes. "I don't think I have any left. On the other hand, if you really wanted it that much why didn't you buy it then?"

"I don't know, madam. A weakness of mine, no doubt. To increase the pleasure of the purchase. Who bought it?"

"What difference does it make?"

"Just to know."

"Some tourist, I think he paid me in dollars."

"Ah!"

"It was very expensive," the woman whispered. "But it was a real beauty."

"It was splendid."

"You really don't like the one in the window?"

"No, madam, I wanted the largest one."

The woman remained silent.

"I know, the difference is minimal," the professor justified himself. "But to me it is crucial."

"Let's see," the woman said turning to the salesman. "The supplier was the Agroppi company, isn't that right?"

"Yes."

"Then, let's go have a look. You can come too," she told the professor.

She walked to the back of the store followed by the professor and the salesman, and then climbed a spiral staircase whose tall steps were carpeted in red. The professor found himself in a huge room lined with industrial shelves full of boxes. The woman went to the window overlooking the arcades and, pointing at the last shelf, told the salesman:

"Try and see if it is up there."

The salesman moved a double ladder in front of the shelves and climbed all the way to the top. Holding on to the last shelf, he stretched the other arm as far as he could toward the pile of boxes and managed to pull out a large green one. As soon as he dangled it in the void, the professor grabbed it. He placed it on a table, opened it, tore off the tissue paper wrapping, and said:

"No. The squares of this board are too shiny. This is not the same wood."

"But that is also rosewood," the salesman said from the top of the ladder.

"Yes, but he means unpolished," the woman intervened.

"That one did not reflect the light," the professor explained, raising his head.

"Right," the woman said. "Natural wood."

The salesman pulled out another box and dangled it over their heads. The professor grabbed it, placed it on top of the other one, and unwrapped it.

"Here," he murmured with glimmering eyes. "This is it."

He frantically ripped the tissue paper wrapping from the board and then ran the fingers of his right hand over its surface:

"See, this is exactly like the other one. The wood is a little coarser and its grains criss-cross."

"What?"

"The grains of the wood in a square should always be perpendicular to those of the wood in the next square."

The woman was dumbfounded.

"I had never thought of it," she said.

"Oh-oh!" the professor suddenly exclaimed. He had lifted the chessboard and was pointing at a corner with his chin:

"Look," he said to the woman.

The woman put her face closer to the board and started examining it. Then she raised her head.

"But it is almost an invisible mark," she said.

"I'm sorry, madam," the professor retorted, wiping sweat off his forehead. "It is quite visible."

"If you hadn't pointed it out to me, I would not have seen it."

"Believe me, madam."

The woman spread her arms in a sign of dismay and looked at the salesman who, at that very moment, exclaimed:

"Here is another one!"

Cradling it in his arms, the professor placed the new box on the table, next to the other two, tore off the tissue paper, and, with a gasp, said:

"Yes, it's the same one."

He pulled it out of the tissue paper and examined it on both sides, running his fingers along its surface. He stopped at a corner.

"This corner is blunted."

The woman touched it, rubbed the end of her thumb against it, then, raising her astonished eyes toward the salesman, said:

"I can't feel a thing."

"Don't you have another one?" the professor asked the salesman.

"No, this is the last one."

"Maybe on some other shelf, in this room."

"I'm sorry, sir," the woman calmly intervened. "This is really the last one."

"What about the supplier?"

"No, sir," the woman patiently said. "The supply has been exhausted. I don't even know if they are going to make them again like that."

"Really?"

"Yes, sir. You can either take this one or do whatever you want. This is the last one. In fact, you can consider yourself lucky."

"Yes."

Readjusting her hair, the woman walked back toward the stairs. A few seconds later, they reappeared, one after the other, in the store.

"Please be careful when you wrap it," the professor told the salesman.

"Shall I leave it in the box?"

"Yes, but wrap it in packing paper."

"We always do, sir," the woman again intervened.

"Fine."

As he stood by the cash register to pay, he kept watching the salesman who, at the other end of the counter, was wrapping the box with packing paper. When he turned it around, although he had tried to be as careful as possible, the box dropped onto the counter.

94

"That's enough," the professor exclaimed, rushing to his side.

"You don't want me to tie it?"

"No, thank you."

He seized the package and tried to hold it under his right arm. But the chessboard was too large. Even holding it just by his fingertips, he would have had to walk awkwardly, bent over toward that side.

He put it back onto the counter and said:

"I can't."

"We can send it to your address," the woman said.

"How?"

"With him," the woman answered pointing at the salesman.

The professor immediately placed both hands on the chessboard. The woman added:

"Don't worry, he won't wreck it."

"No, thank you, madam. I will manage myself."

He again seized the package and tried to hold it horizontally right in front of him, but he had to use both arms, and was forced to keep his chin up. Then, holding it as if in a vice between the index finger and thumb of his right hand, he let it dangle along his side.

"There," he said. "This might work."

Then, walking toward the exit, he added:

"Good evening, madam."

The woman walked him to the door.

"Good evening, sir."

The professor left the store his head held high, but his torso slightly bent to the right. He walked on for a few feet, then, resting the chessboard on his left foot, he stopped and drew a deep sigh. The sunset at the end of the porticoes cast a warm red light onto the stucco vaults. He started walking again, smiling to himself with glittering eyes.

He was happy. Somebody stopped to look at him, but it was only a shadow in the corner of his eye, and it soon disappeared. The cab was just a few feet away.

# IX

Soaked in sweat and exceedingly tired, Daverio caught a glimpse of his own bulging eyes in the mirror above the liquor bottles and, dropping his jaw, stood there glowering at himself as if entranced.

"What would you like, Professor?" the barman asked him.

"A coffee."

"This is your third one this morning."

"I know," Daverio slowly nodded his head. "They are very bad for me."

"I believe you," the barman said, pushing the sugar bowl toward him.

"I feel very shaky."

"So, why do you drink coffee?"

"To feel better, I guess. To perk up my energy."

Outside, the arcades blazed with a white light. He barely made it through the revolving door of the bookstore, before he let himself collapse in a dark corner. He crouched there a while, motionless, eyes closed, hands on knees. By and by the blood flowed back to his head. He opened his eyes and saw a salesman, on top of a ladder, brush the dust off a leather-bound book with a swipe of his palm and tell a student:

"The only Seneca we have is leather bound."

He stood up, approached the window displaying the new titles, and, reflected in the pane against the light, right above the glossy cover of *The Nymphs' Den,* he saw his face looking less drawn. Reassured, he pushed the revolving door to leave. But, stuck between two flaps of the door and looking very elegant with the corner of a handkerchief sticking out of his breast-pocket, Martelli was blocking the mechanism from the outside. As soon as he recognized him, beyond the glass, he backed out onto the steps.

"I'm sorry, I hadn't seen you."

Stiffening his neck, he added:

"How are you? You're not looking so well."

He peered at him with turtle-like eyes.

"Are you going home?"

"Yes."

"If you wait for me by the gate, I'll take you home in a second."

"All right."

Daverio walked slowly toward the arch, through the crowd of students. He stopped by the tower. They were repaving Piazza Risorgimento, and the hot air, rising from the tar, rippled the yellow walls of the barracks.

Martelli's hand landed on his shoulder.

"Come on, tell me what's bothering you," ·he coaxed him, gently steering him toward the opposite end of the square.

"Let's walk a little slower," Daverio said.

They turned into Via Lulli, and followed the

dilapidated walls of Casa Alberti, with the memorial plaque of the *Comune* above the gate and, beyond it, a dilapidated courtyard, all rubble and stones.

"Wait for me here," Martelli said and, making his way through holes and debris, disappeared behind the standing ruins of a wall. Soon after, his car appeared in a cloud of dust, bumping along over the uneven ground. Daverio got into it before it reached Via Lulli.

"How's your thing going?" Martelli asked him. "Still up in the air?"

He turned to look at him while driving slowly.

"Yes, but I'd rather not talk about it."

"Has there been any change since the last time? You told me she gave you reason to hope."

Daverio knit his brow.

"She still does. But I can't take it any longer."

"I can see that."

The car passed under the arch that joined the last two houses of the old town.

"What exactly has she told you?" Martelli asked, while settling into his seat.

"That she feels neither love nor friendship."

"So, what does she feel?"

"She doesn't know."

"And so she is stringing you along," Martelli exclaimed. "Do you still care as much?"

"Yes, I do. But I think I'm having a nervous breakdown."

Lowering his voice, he added:

"It affects my work, everything."

"That doesn't surprise me."

He stopped abruptly at the light.

"I have never seen anyone in such bad shape," Martelli went on. "And what if," he suddenly turned toward him, "she unexpectedly said 'yes.' What would you do?"

"I can't even imagine it."

Martelli steered into Viale della Pace.

"What about her husband? How is he doing?"

"You can easily guess."

Martelli repressed a smile.

"He's probably still recovering from that letter," he said. "Have you seen him?"

"Yes, this morning."

"How was he?"

"Rather depressed."

"I must admit, I'd hate to be in his place."

He stuck his hand out the window, palm up.

"See," he added. "The thing itself is not that important. What matters is what he makes of it."

Daverio stretched out in his seat.

"It has filled his mind with doubts," Martelli continued. "Both about himself and about the writer of the letter."

"That's normal."

The car was slowly ascending the gentle slope of Corso Indipendenza.

"It is quite upsetting to know that somebody hates you," Martelli said. "It's something I have only experienced once in my entire life."

Daverio sat up.

"When?"

"At the beginning of my academic career, from the headmaster of the high school where I taught. At the end of the year I asked to be transferred somewhere else. I couldn't stand it any longer."

"And yet hatred is not such a rare feeling."

"If you can say that, it means that you have never

been hated," Martelli said without turning his head. "Does he suspect anybody?"

"I think he suspects everybody, as you may well imagine. Including me and you, of course."

"Of course!" Martelli exclaimed. "Did he suggest as much to you?"

"No, but I've guessed it all the same."

"What does he say about me?"

"Nothing, we didn't talk about you. How is your relationship with him?"

"Friendly," Martelli answered, straightening his back. "I often hear what he says about me via third parties."

Daverio listened in silence.

"Oh, nothing very direct, of course, you know him. He may bring up the journal I edit, for instance, or some other cultural matter, since it is always done in the name of learning. But we all know what that means, don't we?"

"What does he say?"

"Oh, you can well imagine: he speaks of dilettantism, improvisation. Nothing is ever new to him. His mind is always churning immortal matters, they are his instruments of death."

They had reached Piazza Sempione and were driving along the fence of the public gardens.

"We mostly see each other," Martelli went on, "during the deliberations for the poetry prize."

"What sort of taste does he have?"

"He has an unerring flair for dead things," Martelli answered while stopping at another light. "That's what he likes best."

"How does he defend his position at meetings?"

"With silence."

Then, he added:

"That's exactly it. He says what he has to say and then remains silent for the rest of the meeting. His presumption has no limit and his pride is immense."

Daverio bowed his head.

"That's what I like the most in him."

"And you, what kind of relationship do you have with him?"

Daverio passed a hand over his hair.

"A very peculiar one."

"He doesn't suspect you?"

"You mean about the letter?"

"No, I mean about his wife."

"What should he suspect? There is nothing concrete."

"What do you think about that letter?" Martelli suddenly asked, turning to look at him.

"I could have written it."

"You?"

"Yes."

"No way. I have known you too long," Martelli said, turning his eyes back to the street. "You would never do anything like that."

"Here we are."

Martelli pulled over in front of an early twentieth-century gray stone building. On each side of the front door, two giants bore an enclosed balcony with stained-glass windows on their bent backs. Martelli pointed at it:

"You live in a real fortress."

"You mean in a tomb," Daverio corrected him as he opened his door. "In fact," he leaned back toward him, "you know something I'll never forget? When we entered our bedroom, after our honeymoon, I remember my wife sitting on the bed, saying: 'At last, now we are settled.' And I immediately saw myself in a grave, with both of us building it stone by stone. From that moment on, all I could think of is how to get out of it, at least with my mind."

Martelli was smiling.

"Have you ever noticed how, when we are young, we only talk about building?" Daverio continued. "We are so serious!"

"True."

"And then, after a while, all we want is to destroy, patiently, without sparing anything, and without too much effort either since everything disintegrates in our hands."

Martelli glanced at his watch:

"I'm sorry but it is getting late. I'm expected for lunch."

"You're right," Daverio said, getting out of the car and turning to face the house. "Thank you."

When the elevator reached his apartment, she was already standing in the hallway, ready to open the door.

"How often do I have to ask you to be on time?"

Daverio wiped his forehead with the back of his hand.

"I haven't been feeling well."

"What's the problem?"

"Something I ate this morning."

"So you don't feel like eating now?"

"No."

Daverio went into the bedroom and lay down on the bed, his head on the pillow.

"Take off your clothes, you'll rest more comfortably."

Daverio unbuttoned his shirt and, shrugging his shoulders, let it slide down his arms.

"You've lost a lot of weight."

"I know," he answered, glancing at his ribcage.

"No point asking you what is bothering you. Anyway, you won't tell me."

"But you ask me all the same," Daverio noted as he lay back down. "Maybe I'm having a nervous breakdown. I'm tired of my work."

"But you hardly work."

"That's true," Daverio said, stretching his arms along his sides.

"So that's obviously not the reason."

"I guess not."

She began straightening out the magazines on the desk.

"Can you at least try to give me a sincere answer?"

"Yes."

"Is it because of her?"

"No," Daverio shook his head. "I don't really care any more."

"And yet, every time she calls your mood changes."

"You mustn't be jealous of her. I have already explained everything to you."

He was staring at the chandelier, the palms of his hands turned upwards.

"Is there anything else you want to know?" he asked her.

"Do you see her?"

"Now and then. I saw her yesterday."

"And what do you do together?"

"We talk."

"Of course. She must tell you all about her problems."

She moved away from the desk.

"Can I be sincere with you?"

"No."

"You still haven't lost all your hopes."

"That's right."

"So, why don't you tell me the whole truth?"

"And what would that be?" Daverio had propped himself up on his elbows. "I'm curious."

"Say that you're still in love with her."

She added:

"As you were once, neither more nor less."

Daverio glanced at the ceiling.

"I'm sure you won't believe me," he told her. "But at this point, I hate her."

"Why shouldn't I believe you? You have all the reasons to hate her."

She walked to the window and drew the curtains to the side.

"She has always flattered your vanity, knowing full well how you felt about her. Someone like you waiting for her phone calls!"

Daverio remained silent.

"As for you, it has become an obsession. You have a tendency to fixate on things."

"What does that have to do with it?"

"A lot, because I'm sure it is psychological."

"Everything is psychological."

"True. And you could easily get rid of it. All you'd have to do is get absorbed in your work."

Daverio nodded.

"You're right. I should get back to work."

"And don't answer the phone. I will answer it and tell her that you're not around."

"Not yet. Maybe a little later."

"But will you really do it?"

"Yes."

She approached the bed.

"Are you sure you don't want to eat anything?"

"No. I'd like to lie down here for a while."

He added:

"Thank you. I'll join you in a bit."

As soon as she had closed the door behind her, Daverio looked at his watch, got up, quietly opened the door, then left it ajar. He sat at his desk, picked up the phone, and, craning his neck in the direction of the hallway, started dialing the number. As soon as he heard the ring, he brought his mouth close to the phone.

"Hi," he said, lowering his voice.

"I can't speak any louder," he said. "I don't want her to hear me."

He passed his hand over his forehead.

"I don't know."

Then, abruptly, he said:

"Excuse me."

He turned toward the hallway, and saw a dark spot moving beyond the frosted-glass door. He covered the receiver with a hand and, raising his voice, said:

"Is it you?"

He received no answer, but in the meantime the spot beyond the glass door had disappeared.

"So, you were saying?"

While he was listening, he traced a polygonal figure on a white sheet of paper and then started drawing lines between all its angles.

"Have you had any other dreams?"

He kept doodling.

"What sort of doubts? The usual ones?"

He took another sheet of paper.

"That's all I ever think of."

He hesitated:

"When I'm not thinking of you."

He again glanced at the door.

106

"Yes."

"It's the truth."

He smoothed the paper with the palm of his hand.

"Of course I think of time."

He lowered his head over the paper, and put his eyes close to the drawings.

"You say it's too late? Maybe, I don't know."

He started drawing a series of small circles next to each other.

"Do you remember what Sologùb said to his friend, when he felt that the end was near?"

"I showed you the passage in the bookstore."

"Yes. Hold on a minute."

He got up, went to the small bookcase to the right of the bed, and pulled the second book out of the top row. He opened it at the beginning and picked up the phone.

"Here," he said. "Let me read it to you: 'Only now do I begin to understand life. Why do we understand it only in our old age? And now I must go. Why? For what reason? How do they dare?'"

"Yes."

His eyes were shining.

"Yes. Particularly the last sentence."

"Isn't it?"

He drew a few more lines between the angles of the polygon.

"Me too."

He nodded.

"Very seldom."

Listening, he smiled.

"Of course."

"It's just an expression."

He added:

". . . meaning the opposite."

Suddenly, he said:

"What about your husband?"

He raised his head.

"Because of the letter?"

"I'm sorry."

"Yes, I saw him this morning."

"Exactly."

"What?"

He had suddenly become very pale.

"But the editors won't show it to him."

He shook his head.

"That's not done. Even if he doesn't say who he is. Particularly in that case."

He lifted his face.

"But he is crazy! If he's found out, he could be indicted."

He raised his hand, as if asking for silence, then waited with parted lips. Finally, with a resigned voice, he said:

"I see."

Calmly, he added:

"I realize that."

He swallowed.

"We'll see."

He had started drawing lines between the little circles when the door opened and she walked in with a cup of tea.

"All right."

"Agreed."

"Yes, you can send the book to my home address."

"So long."

He raised his head and whispered:

"Thank you, I really needed something warm."

# X

Holding his chin high and brimming with unexpected energy, the professor strode back to the campus
early that afternoon, passed under the shady arch with
the lion frieze, and confidently looked all the students
he met straight in the eye. On the stone steps that led
to the secretary's office, he saw the assistant and told
him:

"You're the man I was looking for."

"How can I help you, Professor?" the assistant
replied, pirouetting to his left side.

"Who was the student you suspected?"

"Frigerio. I've just seen him."

"Send him to my office."

"What do you mean, Professor?" the assistant stopped
in his tracks. "You knew I wanted to explore the matter
myself."

"I've decided to get to the root of it on my own."

"As you please, Professor."

While the assistant walked down the dark steps, the

professor turned into the hallway, entered his office, and immediately opened the window. Only a few feet away, the cornice of the dome was rimmed with pigeons. He stood there watching their restless movement. Now and then, one of them would take flight and flutter to a landing on the skylight. He leaned on the sill for a long time, until his vacant gaze turned all that stirring into a vitreous mass.

"I just wanted to have a little chat with you," the professor told Frigerio as soon as the assistant had left the office, closing the door behind him.

He added:

"I'll get straight to the point."

The young man watched him with a certain curiosity. The professor leaned back in his chair.

"I am not so sure I should tell you."

"What?"

"However, since you are here. . . have you heard of the piece attacking me?'

"Yes, I have."

"How did you hear about it?"

"I heard Salutati talk about it."

"Where?"

"To Marzano, by the classroom door."

The professor listened to him, aghast.

"Just like that? Out loud?"

"Yes. On the other hand, now that I think of it, I already knew about it."

"Who told you?"

"One of your female students."

"Who?"

Staring at the ground, Frigerio crossed his legs. Then, he said:

"That's not important. I've told you, she is one of your students."

"I see."

The professor stared at him inquiringly.

"Who do you think may have written that letter?"

"One of your colleagues, I suppose."

The professor picked up the letter opener and turned it around in his hands.

"You don't think it could have been a student?"

"No. Absolutely not."

The professor was avoiding his eyes.

"Why?" he asked him.

"Because young people have other things on their minds. As you should know."

"What do you mean?'

With a vaguely ironic smile, Frigerio answered:

"I don't think they are particularly fascinated by the etymology of the word 'hypocrite.'"

"Why not?" the professor asked, and then added:

"I think you are quite wrong there. They are quite interested in the history of words."

"Possibly. But they are not interested in professorial squabbles."

The professor nodded.

"You may be right."

He put the letter opener back on the desk, parallel to the leather case.

"Professor," Frigerio said. "May I ask why you wanted to see me?"

"I've already told you. To have a chat with you."

"But why on that particular subject? I hope you don't suspect one of us."

"Don't be ridiculous!" the professor exclaimed. "I'd never think of that. The idea never crossed my mind!"

Frigerio stared at him.

"Believe me," the professor went on. "I only wanted to exchange a few thoughts with you. What you told me about my colleagues could turn out to be very useful."

He insisted:

"This is the absolute truth. You can believe me. Still, I'd appreciate it if you didn't breathe a word of it to anybody. In other words, don't go around telling everybody."

"I won't."

Standing up, the professor asked him:

"Can I really trust you?"

Frigerio answered with indifference:

"Don't worry."

The professor held out his hand to him:

"So long, then. I expect I'll see you around."

Frigerio quickly shook his hand and immediately proceeded to the door.

As soon as he was gone, the professor clutched his head in his hands and said out loud:

"Why couldn't I stop?"

He took a sheet of paper, crumpled it into a ball, and threw it into the wastebasket. He stifled a sigh.

"Now he is going to tell everybody."

He banged the desk with his fist.

"Why don't I ever do anything right?"

He clutched his head again in his hands.

"Why did I make such a stupid mistake?"


Late that afternoon, in Piazza Famagosta, while the sun, gliding behind the trees, was setting beyond the bleak fields on the outskirts of the city, a cab stopped in front of the *Astrea* building, headquarters of the publishing house. The professor got out, paid the driver, and walked into the marble-floored lobby.

"What are you looking for?" a liveried doorman

asked him, pulling himself away from the column against which he had been leaning.

"*The Voice of Antiquity*," the professor said, and, without waiting for an answer, sneaked through the closing doors of the elevator.

# XI

Locked in a bathroom on the top floor, in front of a little window that opened onto the night and the glitter of streets and buildings, the professor waited. He glanced at the luminous dial of his watch. It was five minutes past one. He stuck his head out the window, into the void, and was barely able to make out the sidewalk of Piazza Famagosta at the bottom of the building, while a large neon sign spelling *Astrea* kept flickering on and off above his head.

He quietly closed the window. Then, he turned the key in the lock and stepped into a dark corridor. He walked lightly along a glassed-in landing until he reached the staircase: tall steps led down to the floor below. Here started another staircase, twice as wide and regularly lit by neon tracks at each landing. Creeping along the wall, the professor checked the floor number engraved on a marble plate at the turn of every ramp. When the plate said 9, he turned left down a long corridor. A yellow light fell from the

115

skylight in the ceiling. To the right of every door, under an oval glass plate, were tags bearing the first and last name of the various occupants: Dionisio D'Amato, Alessio Lessi, Giuseppe Di Marco. Then followed a niche containing a red fire extinguisher and, above it, a button with a notice that said: "Push only in case of emergency."

He followed the corridor to the end. The last name was Ferruccio Moroni. He tiptoed back to the staircase and took the corridor that led in the opposite direction. This side of the building was completely dark. He pulled a tiny flashlight out of his pocket. A circle of red light appeared on the ceiling, turned into an ellipse as it ran down the wall, and then again became a circle at his feet. He walked up to the first white door and aimed the beam at the glass plate. It said: Franco Gerosa. The names by the next few doors were, in this order: Aldo Pontieri, Tina Bas, and Arnaldo Sabbatelli. Around the corner, the first name, in capital letters, was *THE VOICE OF ANTIQUITY*.

The door was not locked. Once in, he ran his hand along the edge of the wall to the right of the door until he found the switch. The fluorescent light flashed on the ceiling, then went off, and then on again. He found himself in a little square room, lined with file cabinets, with a desk in the middle and a typewriter by the window. The tag on the file cabinet to his right read "Correspondence."

He opened the top drawer. The mail was filed according to the month of its arrival in a number of folders that slid along metal tracks. He pulled out the voluminous folder devoted to the month before last and put it on the desk. He rapidly read the beginning of each letter:

Sir:

I have already written you twice to solicit the return of my manuscript. . . .

Dear Professor Amoretti:

Thank you for the space you devoted to Manilio's *Astronomica.* . . .

Dear Sir:

Si licet parva componere magnis. . . .

Gentlemen:

Is it possible. . . .

Dear Professor:

I have never pretended that my research was exhaustive. . . .

Dear Amoretti:

Following our phone conversation, why not devote an entire issue to Nigidius Figulus, magician and philosopher. . . .

Half a page down, he spotted the word "naked," but it referred to truth: "the naked truth is that the question of the saturnian line hasn't yet been satisfactorily answered."

Gentlemen:

Am I supposed to interpret your silence as. . . .

Dear Amoretti:

As Macchiavelli justly said once: *"Sendo l'intento mio scrivere cosa utile a chi la intende.. . .*

117

Dear Sir:

Hypocrisy is the water in which we all swim: it keeps us afloat all our life, and, in the end, sinks us. . . .

*Professor Ettore Pasini*
*Viale Rainusso 32*
*Santa Margherita Ligure*

(please do not mention the name of the sender)

The professor leaned his hands on the desk. He felt short of breath. He did not know any Ettore Pasini. Nor had he ever been in Santa Margherita Ligure. He reread the letter. As far as he could remember, it was identical to the one that had been published. He pulled a white sheet of paper from his pocket and wrote down the name and address. Then he put the letter back with the other ones. As he went over to the file cabinet, his legs were seized by a sudden tremor. He felt drained, from the waist down, as if his veins were emptying out. He leaned against the desk with his hands, his legs wide apart, his chest heaving in slow motion. For some reason or other, he remembered a frog he had seen on television: a huge close-up of a swelling throat and bulging eyeballs. He had to sit down.

When he got up, he made sure that everything was exactly the way he had found it. He turned the wastebasket that he had accidentally knocked over right side up, switched off the lights, and walked out.

He tiptoed to the landing and proceeded down the stairs. He had already reached the sixth floor when he missed a step. Clutching the banister with one hand, he managed to soften his fall with the other. But the noise echoed all the way down the stairwell. He remained in a huddled position, motionless. After a short wait, he scrambled to his feet and started down again, holding on to the banister with both hands. On the third floor, he left the banister and pressed his hands against the green stucco wall. He stopped by a velvet sofa over which hung the notice: "All visitors must wait to be announced."

Then, he quietly descended the last flights of stairs, but a few steps away from the floor of the lobby he again stopped. He felt two eyes staring at him from below.

"What are you doing here?" the night watchman asked.

Instinctively, he turned around and, without answering, hurried back upstairs, more and more rapidly and increasingly out of breath.

"Stop!" the watchman shouted.

On the second floor, the professor rushed into the corridor to his left. He tried a door but it was locked. He rounded the corner, but after a few steps, he stopped. He was panting, his hands hung limply by his sides.

He turned on his heels, ran his hand through his hair, readjusted the knot of his tie, and walked back toward the staircase. Immediately around the corner, a hand grabbed his arm:

"Who are you ?"

"Let go of me," the professor said wresting his arm free.

The watchman grabbed it again.

"Not so fast. I want to know what you are doing here."

"Please, try to understand," the professor said stopping and gazing straight into his eyes. "You have the wrong idea. Let me explain everything."

Tightening his hold, the night watchman led him toward the stairs. He even gave him a little push and the professor, with a long shudder, had to hold on to the banister not to fall.

"Please, let's try to understand each other," the professor implored.

"Right now, you're coming with me," the watchman retorted.

Once in the lobby, he pushed him toward the doorman's office.

"Stay seated while I call," he said and picked up the phone.

"No, please," the professor insisted, seizing his arm. "First you have to give me a chance to explain."

Holding the receiver in his hand, the watchman looked at him.

"All right," he said. "But do it fast."

"I can see why you would suspect me," the professor began. He felt his voice thicken and his eyes tingle. "But I am not a thief."

"What are you then?"

"I can't tell you that," the professor answered, bowing his head. "But I'm not a thief."

"I'm going to call the police," the watchman said and started to dial the number.

"Please, wait," the professor still hesitated. He had begun to sweat. "Can I trust you?"

"So, now you're asking if you can trust me?"

Clasping his hands together, the professor pleaded with him:

"You have no idea of the scandal it would create if it were known," he said. "My whole career is at stake, you understand?"

The watchman looked at him with perplexed eyes.

"I know how to show my gratitude," the professor stuttered.

He slipped a hand into his jacket to pull out his wallet, but the watchman stopped him.

"Don't bother, I don't go for that sort of thing."

The professor readjusted his glasses without saying a word.

"I warn you, I'm the last person you want to try that stuff on."

The professor sat down.

"I did not come here to steal."

"In that case, why did you come?"

"To look for a letter attacking me, a letter that was published."

"So, why did you need to look for it?"

"Because they omitted the name of the writer. I wanted to know who had written it. That's why I waited until they locked the building."

The watchman put the receiver down and looked at him with suspicion.

"Show me some identification."

"No," the professor answered, automatically covering the left side of his jacket with his open hand.

"If I were you I wouldn't make me lose my patience," the watchman had moved closer. "If you want me to trust you, you must trust me first."

"Yes," panting, the professor agreed. "Yes, you're right."

He pulled the wallet out of the inside pocket of his jacket, gently drew his I.D. card out, and handed it to the watchman.

The watchman opened it, examined the picture, and then looked up at at him.

"Don't move," he said.

He walked around the table and went to a shelf. There, he held the I.D. card against the wall and started copying its number on a sheet of paper.

"What are you doing?" the professor asked, jumping up from his chair.

"I told you not to move," the watchman said, turning his back on him to hide what he was writing. The professor tried to tear the paper away from him, but the other shoved him away. The professor clung to the edges of the table and managed to stay on his feet in the middle of the room. He saw the watchman copy his name, date and place of birth, his address, and profession. Then, he handed the card back to him:

"Now you can have it back."

Putting it back into his wallet with trembling hands, the professor asked him:

"What are you going to do with it?"

"Don't you worry," the watchman replied, sitting down. "I must take my precautions."

The professor also sat down.

"You are not thinking of reporting me to the police."

"It depends," the watchman replied. As he folded the paper and slipped it in his pocket, he kept his eyes on him. "It depends on you."

"Meaning?" the professor asked, placing his hands on the table.

"I have to make sure that what you told me is true," the watchman pushed his chair back. "Just to play it safe, you see."

"Yes," the professor mumbled.

"One never knows, don't you agree?"

"Does this mean that you don't believe me?"

"I do, I do, otherwise I wouldn't be listening to you. No need to be so upset. Calm down."

The professor's voice grew pleading:

"I am calm," he said. "But I can't quite understand what you intend to do."

"I can assure you that if you have done nothing wrong nothing will happen."

"You want to drive me crazy," the professor went on. "I am already going through a horrible time."

"What the hell do you expect from me," the watchman said, standing up. "You should thank heaven I'm not going to report you to the police."

"Yes."

The professor stood up.

"You should thank heaven you ran into me."

"Yes."

"So. Now you can go," and he showed him the door.

Pale, trembling, and with a pounding heart, the professor stole out of the doorman's office and staggered toward the exit.

# XII

Finally alone in his apartment, while the elevator was taking his wife downstairs, Daverio gently locked the door and walked back to his room. He pulled his large tape recorder out of its leather case and placed it on the desk. Then, sitting down, he pressed the *rewind* button. Leaning his head on the palm of his right hand, he watched the tape spin between the two spools. When it had almost entirely rewound onto the left spool, he stopped it.

He got up to close the door and, walking to the window, drew the curtains aside. He saw his wife on the opposite sidewalk looking up at him. He nodded at her and she smiled. He let the curtains drop, went back to his desk, sat down, and pressed the *play* button. He heard the telephone ringing.

Then her voice:

"Hello?"

"Hi, it's me."

"Ah, it's you!?"

He pressed the *rewind* button and then again the *play* button.

"Ah, it's you!?"

He pressed the *stop* button. It was her usual tone of voice, mixing joy and surprise, and yet there was a new inflection to that "Ah."

He pressed the same buttons:

"Ah, it's you!?"

It sounded as if she had been impatiently waiting for his call. . .

He pressed the same buttons again:

"Ah, it's you!?"

. . . and were now reproaching him for having taken so long.

He pressed *rew*, then the second speed button, and then again *play*. The tape slackened, wiggled, and then gradually stretched out again:

"Aaaahhhh, iiiittttssss yyyyooooouuuu!?!?!?!?"

He pressed the first speed button, for the slowest speed, but all he got was a prolonged raucous rattle.

He remembered her sulking as she waited for him near the newspaper stand, in Viale Romagna:

"This is the second time you've arrived late for our meetings."

He pressed *rew*, and then the third speed button.

"Hello?"

"Hi, it's me."

"Ah, it's you!?"

"Yes, are you sorry?"

He pressed *stop*.

"Why am I so dumb?" he muttered.

He pressed *play*.

"Not a bit. You know I'm always glad to hear your voice."

"Really?"

He pressed *stop* again. That anxious reply was another mistake. And that was not all. He pressed *play.*

"Of course."

"You really mean it?"

He pressed *stop.* He contemplated the unwound tape between the two spools. Why did he have to behave like an adolescent? Begging for an inevitably disappointing answer rather than knowing when to shut up.

He pressed *play.*

"Yes. You know it—do you have a moment?"

"Yes."

He again stopped the tape. Even that "yes," so feeble and compliant—one could intuit the smile that went with it—was a mistake.

He stood up and said, out loud:

"Of course, darling."

It left him thoughtful, his hands on the desk, staring at the lamp in the corner.

"Of course, darling," he repeated with a calmer voice, nodding.

"Of course," he added.

This time, his voice sounded absent-minded, almost indifferent. Smiling, he looked at the curtains.

"Of course, darling."

Yes, that was it, no need to fake it. The tone had to be natural, with a warm timbre.

"Of course, darling," he again repeated, still smiling.

He sat with a bowed head in front of the recorder.

He pressed the *play* button.

"You are always so patient. Aren't you ever tired of me?"

"No."

He again stopped the tape and got up. Why did he have to sound so pathetic, so moved?

"Wrong again! You should have told her!" he exclaimed. "Yes! Of course I'm tired of you. I'm exhausted!"

That's how he should have answered. Exaggerating the truth in order to utter it. Pretending he was joking when, in fact, with her, he had never been able to pretend, nor to joke.

"As a matter of fact, I can't even listen to you any longer," he added.

But he could only muster that tone when he was particularly euphoric.

"Do you understand?" he asked, addressing the wall.

"Yes," she would have answered, laughing as she was wont to do on the rare occasions when he pretended to be offended.

"I have had it with all your doubts and your reticence."

"You're being terrible," she would have told him.

"That's right."

No, that was not the right thing to say.

"Yes, I am!" he had to insist since this was a perfect occasion and she was listening to him with great curiosity, without trying to dodge the issue (as she had done the last time, not without some embarrassment, when, in Via Tadino, he had broached the subject of their relationship): "I don't mind talking literature with you, or even helping you deal with your doubts."

"But?"

"But the most essential thing for me . . . you can imagine what that is."

"Yes, I can," she would have answered, "but I don't want to hear it."

"But you must."

He stared at the chandelier with teary eyes. He should not speak of his feelings but rather of what she was in his eyes. Nor should he accompany his compliments with a smile, as if begging for her indulgence. Even the most daring ones he should utter in utmost seriousness. Only this way would he acquire authority without leaving her room for false objections.

He sighed and slowly turned his head. He was sure that at that particular moment she would not have interrupted him, would not have digressed. So, why wasn't he able to talk to her like that while they were walking along the boulevards, near the stadium, and, why, instead of fixing his eyes on hers, did he prefer to look elsewhere? Those images still pierced his pupils, he saw them that clearly, and he could still feel her presence by his side, but he could not remember her face. Instead, he could remember perfectly the steps of the stadium, the stands, the box offices, the outer gate.

"That I should fall so in love at my age."

No. That would have been a mistake. That was his own private thought—besides, she could have replied and that had to be prevented.

He sat down. Pressed a button. For a while, he just sat there staring at the turning tape, as if lulled by its rustle. What had he done? He immediately interrupted the recording. He had pressed the wrong button, and was erasing his phone call.

"Oh!" he screamed.

He struck the desk with his fist, and passed the back of his hand over his sweaty forehead.

Then he pressed *play*.

". . . me to tell you the last news?"

"I am listening."

129

"He has found out who wrote that letter. His name is Pasini, and he teaches in Santa Margherita."

"How did he do that?"

"Three nights ago, he went to the publishing house and let himself be locked up in the building. Unfortunately a watchman saw him and took down his name."

"What?"

"Yes. He hasn't slept a wink for the last two nights. Now he is afraid he might be blackmailed. I've never seen him in such a state. Believe me, I'm quite worried."

"What about this Pasini? Who is he?"

"He's a complete stranger whose name he has never heard before. But he is afraid he might be well informed, and know a great deal about him, and that one day he might decide to expose him."

"That's right."

"What do you mean 'that's right'?"

"Nothing. I was listening to what you were saying."

"No. You are hiding something from me."

"Not at all."

"You swear?"

"I swear."

"That's not enough. I'm not convinced."

"But why?"

"Because you sounded as if you found it perfectly natural that Pasini would want to expose him ."

"I didn't find it natural at all. Don't put words in my mouth."

"Why are you such a hypocrite?"

"A hypocrite?! Me?! With you!?"

"Yes, with me. You are not telling me the truth."

"How do you know?"

"I sense it, I can tell from the tone of your voice,

from what you say. And please, spare me your usual digressions on truth."

"Do you care that much?"

"About what?"

"About him."

"Of course I do."

"And what about me?"

He stopped the tape and got up. Groaning through his teeth, he lay down on the bed and closed his eyes. The wail that echoed in his ears thinned down to a whine and gradually faded away. When he opened his eyes, he saw the alabaster chandelier hanging right above his face. Between the center and the circumference of the main globe there were two oddly regular streaks that reminded him of the stylized thunderbolts painted on electric poles, tips dipping into a pink cloud.

He got up and returned to the recorder. He pressed the *rewind* button, and then *play*.

". . . are that much?"

"About what?"

"About him."

"Of course I do."

"And what about me?"

He pressed *stop* again and sat down. Why did he ask her then? At the worst possible moment? Instead of waiting for the conversation to turn playful, when he could have easily asked her, with a smile:

"And what about me?"

Raising his voice he repeated:

"And what about me?"

But that was a real question, a question that demanded an answer rather than suggesting, or presupposing, one.

He knit his brow pensively and then murmured:

"And what about me?"

He smiled:

"And what about me?"

That was it. All he had to do was smile affably. But then, if he knew that, why did he keep botching it?

He turned the volume all the way down, so as not to hear anything at all, and then pressed *play*. The tape slowly unwound and then stretched out again. Only the whirr of the motor was audible. At this point she should have finished talking, and he should have started answering her. He raised the volume.

". . . all you think of."

He again turned down the volume. She was delivering a long speech that he did not feel like hearing again: the same old formulas that meant exactly the opposite of what they said.

He turned the volume up. She was saying:

"Believe me, I have no doubts about my feelings."

"That's not true," he said out loud.

He had stopped the tape.

"Admit it," he added. "Acknowledge it."

He pressed *play*.

"I am always full of doubts, but not in this matter."

"Sure you aren't," he muttered, staring at the tape. He pressed *stop* and walked into the hallway. He hesitated a while between the bathroom and the kitchen and then went into the latter. He opened the refrigerator and poured half a can of beer into a glass on the table. It was ice cold. He wiped his mouth with his hand and, back in the bedroom, he let himself fall spread-eagled onto the bed. The light coming in from the window had dimmed. Suddenly there was a flash of lightning, and, immediately after, the rumble of a thunder rattled the windowpanes. Daverio got up and went to the window. Dark clouds drifted above the houses, while the wind shook the poplars of the race-track. A few large drops were quickly followed by a crashing downpour. He saw his wife running from the sidewalk across the street in the direction of the house, looking up at him, and covering her head with her leather handbag.

He went back to the recorder and switched it off.

# XIII

Wavering between two pastries of equal size, a Napoleon with a thick crust of icing sectioned into squares and a sort of St. Honoré topped by a multiple crown of cream puffs culminating in a large strawberry, the customer, with a prim goatee and a sizable pot-belly squeezed under his vest, looked up at the salesgirl and asked her:

"Which one should I buy?"

"It depends on your tastes."

"Yes, I know. But which one would you choose?"

"I would choose this one," and she pointed at the Napoleon. "I'm devouring it with my eyes."

"You are, hmm?" the customer smiled.

"No joke," the salesgirl answered. "I have a very sweet tooth."

The customer placed his briefcase by his feet in front of the bright display window.

"How can you resist in a pastry shop?"

"I often wonder," the salesgirl sighed. "And yet I manage."

"I can see that."

"Without losing my figure," the salesgirl added.

"I can also see that," the customer replied, looking at her. "How do you do it?"

"It's a huge sacrifice, sir," the salesgirl answered. "But well worth the effort."

"No doubt about that," the customer agreed. "You look well."

"Thank you. You no longer fight to keep up your figure?"

"Oh yes," the customer answered. "Daily. But, as you can see, without much success."

The salesgirl laughed.

"So, would you like your pastry in a box?"

"Yes, " the customer answered. "Please."

Outside the wind had gained in strength and was bending the palm trees landward. The street was wet with the spray of waves crashing against the rocks. He walked under the low, damp vaults of the arcades, through wafts of fried food and fresh fruit. In the small square he turned into a street with steps that climbed up between two rows of very tall houses. At the top, past a short gallery, he emerged into the sunlight on a small balcony overlooking the sea. Holding the railing with both hands, he stared at the shimmering expanse dotted with sailboats. Then he pulled his watch chain out of his vest pocket and headed up a winding street toward a pink villa, half-hidden by palmettos.

The gate was open. He followed the gravel path up to the steps that led to the pillared porch and the front door. A barking dog rushed out of the park behind the

136

house and started scampering up and down the steps in front of him until it was shushed by the maid.

"Be quiet, Flick, don't you see it's only Professor Pasini."

"He's just happy to see me," Pasini said patting the dog's back as it briskly wagged its tail. "Let him be."

Shivering all over, the dog whined with pleasure. Pasini patted it one more time and then entered a cool, bright veranda, while the maid closed the door at his back and told him:

"I am going to call Francesca."

Pasini sat by the window at a table on which a leather-bound Latin dictionary and a steaming teapot had already been placed.

"You like yours without milk, right, Professor?" another maid asked him, entering the veranda.

"Yes, please."

Francesca appeared shortly thereafter in a tennis outfit and carrying a pile of books that came up to her chin.

"You should be proud of me, Professor. I've even studied Livy."

"That's very good. And did you translate every sentence?"

"Yes, I did. They drove me nuts," the girl answered putting the pile of books on the table. "One would think you are trying to teach me Latin by writing an almost incomprehensible Italian."

"Read me the first sentence."

"Here it is," the girl said opening a notebook. " 'I don't know what would have happened to me if I had promised to return before you.' "

"And now read me your translation."

" '*Nescirem quod mihi venturus sit si promisissem redire ante te.*' "

137

"Well, well," Pasini said. He pulled his watch out of his vest pocket and placed it on the table in front of him.

It was two past ten. The windowpanes vibrated lightly at each gust of the wind that blew in from the sea tousling the tips of the palm trees.

"Well, well," Pasini repeated. "There are at least five mistakes."

"I swear I felt it coming!" the girl said.

At five past eleven, Pasini got up to leave, and the girl accompanied him to the gate. He retraced his steps down to the little balcony and under the leaky gallery, then he turned right and found himself in the crowded fish market. Fending his way through the screams and crates of the fishmongers, he turned off into a narrow side street flanked by orange houses, and then onto a tree-lined avenue whose villas rose from below street level. Short bridges connected them to small wrought-iron gates. Halfway down the avenue, to the right, was a row of shops. Pasini crossed the street and entered a small used-book store. The owner was just returning from the storage cellar through a trapdoor in the floor of the shop. Pasini helped him out and then asked him:

"No news about Paul de Kock's *Memoirs?*"

"Hopefully yes, Professor," the owner replied, smoothing his jacket and closing the wooden trapdoor at his back. "I might be able to get them for you by the end of the month. Do you know where I found them?" he asked as he banged a book against the edge of his desk to let out the dust. "In a catalog of Romantic literature. And here I thought he was a scientist!"

"You might have confused him with Robert Koch."

"Whatever, Professor. You'll have your book by the end of the month."

"Thank you very much," Pasini said, leaving the store.

A few steps down the tiled sidewalk, he opened the gate of a three-story house smothered in ivy, crossed the little bridge, and descended to the first floor apartment, a few feet below the level of the street.

"Who is it?" the voice of a little girl asked from the inside.

"It's me. Your aunt isn't back yet?"

"No," the little girl answered as she opened the door. She could barely reach the handle.

She added:

"A gentleman is waiting for you in the other room."

"Who?"

"I don't know, he didn't say."

"I'll go see. This is for dinner."

He pulled the pastry box out of the bag and bent down to hand it to her. Smiling, the little girl clapped her hands and then, holding the box in both hands as if it were a tray, brought it to the kitchen.

Pasini entered the study. A small man in his fifties, with unusually thick lenses, immediately got up from his armchair.

"I must apologize for this unexpected visit," he said. "But I believe you know me."

"I know you?" answered Pasini, surprised, shaking his hand. "No, I don't think so. But, please, sit down."

He noticed that the other man kept staring at him as he sat down, and that his right hand, leaning on the armrest, trembled.

"I'm afraid," Pasini smiled, "I don't remember you. On the other hand, I have always had trouble remembering faces. Did we by chance meet in the service?"

"I don't think so," the other answered, extraordinarily pale. "But, please, allow me a little time before I satisfy your curiosity. It won't take long. Would you mind?"

"As you wish," Pasini answered, somewhat perplexed, as he also sat down.

"In fact, would you be so kind as to let me ask you a few questions first?"

"As you please," Pasini answered, increasingly baffled.

"You are interested in historical linguistics, is that correct?"

"Yes," Pasini answered. "But only as an amateur. How do you know?"

"You are not an expert?"

"No. I teach classics at the Liceo Vittorino da Feltre. Linguistics fascinates me, as do many other fields. That's all."

"You don't write?"

"Yes, a few articles for the local papers, on the origins and history of Ligurian names, for instance. Nothing very important."

"Do you, by any chance, know the book *Nomina Numina?*"

"Indeed, I do. A wonderful book. One of the most interesting texts I have ever read. I even own a copy," and he pointed at a shelf above the professor's head.

"Do you know its author?"

"Not personally. But I would like to."

"Ah, you would like to," the other repeated, suddenly breathing with difficulty. "You respect him."

"Of course I do."

The professor squinted at him.

"And yet, you write quasi-anonymous letters attacking him."

"Me?" Pasini exclaimed staring at him. "What are you saying? Anyway, who are you?"

"Answer me," the other muttered through his teeth. "Did you or didn't you write a letter attacking him?"

"I didn't."

"Are you sure?"

"I've told you, I didn't. Don't push me or I'll lose my patience."

"And so will I," the other said slowly. "You are a liar!"

At first, Pasini was dumbfounded. Then he clutched the armrests of his chair and made as if to lunge at the professor. But, in a flash of overlapping images, he saw a tilted armchair, a shattered liquor cabinet, the little girl rushing in from the hallway.

"You don't know what you are saying," he gasped, getting up and approaching his visitor's chair. "You haven't even told me who you are. But, in any case, out of this house!"

"I'm going to tell you," the other answered without getting up, and staring straight ahead. "You really don't know who I am?"

He glanced at Pasini, hovering over him, then went on:

"I am the author of *Nomina Numina*."

"What!?"

Pasini was now struck by a different kind of wonder that made him feel unsteady on his legs.

"You?!"

He walked back to his chair and sat down.

"What do you mean?"

Still incredulous, he added:

"This must be a case of mistaken identity."

"I wish that were true," the other said.

"But it is!" Pasini exclaimed. "I have never written a word attacking you. You must believe me."

The professor gazed at him in silence.

"You must be the victim of a misunderstanding," Pasini continued. "You believe I wronged you."

"Precisely."

"This is absolutely crazy! I only know you through your books."

"Then how do you justify your letter?"

"What letter?"

Exhausted, Pasini leaned his head against the back of his chair. The professor, meanwhile, was rapidly recovering his spirits.

"The letter you wrote to *The Voice of Antiquity*."

"I have never written a letter to that journal."

"Can I really believe you?"

"I give you my word of honor."

The professor, still hesitant, scrutinized him. He pulled a large handkerchief from his pocket and wiped his forehead. Then, he said:

"My God."

He passed a hand over his face.

"God," he repeated.

Then he looked at his host with dismay:

"If that's really the case, please, forgive me."

"I do," Pasini murmured, his arms dangling over the sides of his chair.

"And yet I have seen the letter with your name and address."

"With my signature?"

"Yes, though it was illegible."

"Impossible. My signature has always been very clear," Pasini said, shaking his head. "If you want to see it, I'll show it to you."

"Never mind, it's no longer important."

142

But Pasini had already gotten up and, having pulled out of his desk a manuscript titled "Rapallo: rea palus?" was now showing him the signature at the bottom of the fourth page:

"Is this the signature you saw?"

"No. It is clearly a trap," the other answered, barely glancing at it.

He closed his eyes and added:

"How is such a thing possible?"

"I can't imagine," Pasini answered, returning to his chair. "What did the letter contain."

"All sorts of perfidious insinuations."

"And they published it under my name?"

"No. They published it with the name and address withheld."

Pasini emitted a sigh of relief. Then he asked:

"And it bothers you a great deal?"

"Yes, I can't possibly deny that."

"Obviously, given your position, you must have quite a few enemies."

"But this is a little different," the professor said, softly. "This is someone who really wants to harm me, who wants to stab me in the back."

Pasini frowned:

"I wonder why he chose my name."

In the meantime, the little girl had poked her head through the door. Looking at the guest with uncertainty, she muttered:

"Auntie's back."

"All right. But now leave us alone."

Pasini got up and walked her to the hallway, gently pushing her by the shoulders.

When he returned, the professor, who in the meantime had stood up, said:

"Maybe the author of the letter is someone who knows you."

"Hmm," Pasini answered without much conviction, keeping his eyes on the floor. "I really don't think so."

"Maybe he found your name in the telephone book. He must have been looking for the name of a real professor, with a real address, so as to remain above suspicion."

"Still it is strange that he should have picked my name."

"Yes, it is strange," the professor said, hanging his head and walking toward the door. "I don't believe anything ever happens by chance. But it isn't always easy to find the right connections. Anyway. . ."

Pasini looked thoughtful.

"I'll explain everything to you as soon as I get to the bottom of this whole story," the professor went on. "I mean, of this nightmare."

He walked toward the hallway, then he turned around. He took Pasini's hand between both of his:

"Once again, I must beg you to forgive me."

"Don't even think of it," Pasini answered as he walked him to the door.

"I'll send you one of my books with a dedication," the professor went on. "Have you read my essay 'Origines'?"

"No, not yet."

"Good, I will send it to you."

He climbed the steps ahead of Pasini. On the bridge, he turned around one more time to tell him:

"I count on your discretion. And, once again, please forgive me."

Opening the gate for him, Pasini asked:

"Do you have to leave immediately?"

"Yes. I would love to stay, but it is late," the professor answered with absent eyes. "Maybe one day we'll meet again."

Pasini remained silent.

As the professor walked away, Pasini stood motionless by the gate. He could have turned around and walked down the steps and back into the house, where he could have told his sister everything that had happened. But he did not feel like talking. Instead, he walked down the sidewalk, under the plane trees, along the half-deserted street. A continuous shiver ran through his body. That unexpected meeting had shaken him. Hardly twenty minutes ago he had never seen that man's face. Then, he had met him, he had almost punched him, and now it was all over.

He kept walking down the sidewalk, mulling over the images of that meeting, feeling unusually restless, anxious. Everything seemed so fortuitous. Why had the professor said that nothing ever happened by chance?

He knew he would never see him again.

# XIV

Perched on two aluminum stools, the professor and the girl were drinking an aperitif at the chrome-plated, horseshoe counter of the bar located on top of the hill in the center of the park. The professor, whose feet could not reach the floor, stretched his hand toward the bowl of olives. Then, blowing his nose, he emitted a strange noise and asked her:

"Did you bring your poems?"

"Yes."

The professor gazed at the bottles lined up behind the bar and then at the bottom of his glass.

"Are you in a hurry?" the girl asked him.

"No," the professor answered, glancing at his watch.

He hesitated:

"Is half an hour enough?"

The girl blushed:

"Even less. You are the one who said you had time."

"You're right," the professor said, emptying his

glass. "I'd forgotten that this evening I'm supposed to see Cattaneo; I want to get his advice about my reply."

"Your reply to the letter? So you have decided to answer?"

"Yes."

"Why are you going to see him?"

"He is an expert on language, particularly other people's. When it comes to his own writing, he isn't worth that much.

The girl listened to him, perplexed.

"Don't you think you are exaggerating a bit?" she asked him.

The professor did not answer.

"There was something else I wanted to ask you," the girl added, putting her glass down on the counter.

"What?"

"I've forgotten. Let me think for a second."

The professor rested his elbow on the counter and stared at her.

"No, really, I no longer know what I wanted to say," the girl continued. "Anyway, the gist of it was that you are spending too much time obsessing on that letter. You're putting your entire past into question."

"You mean, my future."

Nonplussed, the girl stole a glance at him.

"Whatever," she said.

Then, on second thought, she added:

"Maybe it's the same: your past is also your future. Am I making any sense?"

"No."

"What I mean is that you must not feel so implicated in it. It is not the sort of thing that should push you to the brink."

"You might be right," the professor muttered.

"There is nothing as fatal as lending credence to one's enemies."

"Why, you believe them?"

"No, but I can't ignore them."

The girl was about to reply, but the professor went on:

"I would like to know who did it because I would like to confront him with it. To be attacked is bad enough, but to be shunned because your enemy despises you is even worse. If I could meet him face to face, talk to him, everything would be different."

"But this is precisely your greatest weakness," the girl said turning her face up at him. "You would like to convince him."

The professor stared at her.

"Believe me, it's childish," the girl continued. "This constant need to convince others, everybody, that you are right, that you are better than they are. You should try to imagine, at least once, what it would be like to be in the opposite situation, to be wrong. What would happen? Would the world cave in? Besides, I cannot understand how, at your age, you can still be a slave to other people's opinions."

The professor remained silent for a while and then said:

"Maybe you are right. I should abandon all polemics. Is this what you mean?"

"Exactly," the girl exclaimed. "If I were you I wouldn't even bother to answer."

"And yet, not long ago, you believed I should."

"I did?"

The girl gulped down her aperitif:

"Obviously, I can no longer remember why I said that, but I must have had my reasons. Anyway, it no

149

longer matters. What matters is how you're going to react now."

The professor nodded.

"If I could always be as calm as I am now, as detached," he said.

"See, you already look better," the girl exclaimed. "You've got to get rid of this obsession."

"Yes, what you just said might help."

"And now, do you feel like having a look at my poems?"

"Yes," the professor said, sliding off his stool. "Let's go outside, what do you think?"

He pointed at the panoramic terrace, overlooking the foliage of the park.

"Great," the girl answered. She grabbed her shoulder bag from the counter and joined him at the door.

"You really feel like it?"

"Yes, I've told you," the professor answered, pushing the glass door open.

"Won't mood influence you?" the girl again asked, passing in front of him while he held the door open for her.

"No, I'm feeling much better now. Where shall we sit?"

"Down there," the girl answered, pointing at the swing in a corner of the terrace.

The tiled floor was still wet from the recent storm. They were the only two people out there. Weaving through the empty tables the girl was the first to sit on the swing's cushions.

"Oh, it's all wet!" she exclaimed without getting up.

"Then I won't sit down," the professor said, bending under the canopy and patting the fabric of the cushions.

150

"Just a touch, I swear." The girl seized his hand and led it to a spot near her leg. "See?"

"Yes, but mine is damper than yours."

"Then let's trade them."

"No, wait."

He went to a swing that was leaning against the wall and took one of its cushions. Bending again under the canopy, he then placed it on top of the wet one.

"Now you're literally towering over me," said the girl.

"Indeed, my head is touching the top," the professor smiled, glancing at the colored canvas right above his eyes. Meanwhile, the girl had pulled a rolled manuscript out of her bag. As she was trying to uncurl the pages, the professor asked her:

"May I?"

"Yes," the girl answered, letting go of the manuscript.

"This is your only copy?"

"No, I have another one that I must hand in to the Prize Committee before Saturday."

"So we don't have to worry about marking this up?" the professor said flattening the manuscript out on his knees.

"Not at all. In fact, I'd like to have your corrections."

She pulled a pen from her bag and handed it to him:

"I'd be very grateful."

The trees of the avenue, below, reached the top of the parapet with their wet foliage. The professor planted his feet firmly on the tiles of the floor to keep the seat from swinging and glanced at the sun setting above the park, amidst red tattered clouds. Then he adjusted his glasses on the bridge of his nose and started reading.

At his right, the girl watched him, holding on to her cushion with both hands. The professor's face grew graver and graver, then it looked up and remained perfectly still and utterly expressionless.

"So?" the girl asked, blushing. "Don't worry, I am ready for the worst."

Turning halfway toward her, the professor asked:

"You just wanted me to see the second one, right?"

"Yes."

The professor remained silent. The girl asked him:

"What didn't you like?"

"Well, just about everything."

He avoided looking at her.

"I don't like the general tone," he added, resting his hand on top of the manuscript. "Besides, who is this 'thou' you are addressing?"

"That has nothing to do with anything," the girl retorted. "Anyway, it is not you."

"It has nothing to do with your poem either."

"Why?"

"It doesn't tie in with the rest, it remains totally extraneous to the poem, whoever it is and wherever it comes from."

The girl was pouting at the floor.

"But I wanted it that way."

"I believe you," the professor said. "But that might not be enough for your readers. Many texts correspond exactly to what their authors wanted them to be, but that is often their greatest problem."

"You mean to tell me that it would be better not to know what we are doing?"

"Not at all. You know exactly what I mean," said

the professor, letting the chair swing. "To express one's thoughts is not enough, first one must think."

"So, you think originality is irrelevant?"

The professor pulled himself up on his cushion:

"Are you nervous?" he asked her.

The girl shrugged slightly.

"I don't believe in originality the way you understand it," the professor continued. "It must be a discovery but also a reconfirmation, otherwise it would be monstrous. As in the instance of that father who gave his terminally ill daughter a gorgeous coffin for her birthday. It was an undeniably original present which neither his daughter nor anyone else would have ever expected, but it was also the gift of a madman."

"No doubt about it," the girl murmured. "But, how did we get to talking about coffins?"

The professor did not answer. The girl went on:

"As usual, you have digressed. Let me turn my question around. Is there anything you like in this poem?"

The professor hesitated and then looked at the manuscript.

After a long pause, he said:

"Well, for instance, I don't mind the inversion 'sunset and dawn' in the third line. One would normally expect to read 'dawn and sunset,' sort of like 'the Ancients and the Moderns,' whereas you say 'the Moderns and the Ancients,' or rather 'sunset and dawn.'"

Dissatisfied with his answer, he turned to look at her:

"I'm not so sure I have explained myself clearly."

"What interests you always leaves me perplexed,"

the girl said. "It is always so different from what interests me."

The professor looked again at the manuscript.

"Actually, the intrusion of that obscene word in the first line is quite effective," he said. "Which does not mean it is good. The effect in itself does not mean anything. Try to repeat a disgusting word five times and you'll see what happens to your disgust. And that's true for any word. Try 'sky,' for instance. You'll see how odd it can sound."

He turned toward her and, in an even tone of voice, repeated:

"Sky, sky, sky, sky, sky."

The girl listened with lowered eyes.

The professor went on:

"On the other hand, this first line might work better at the end, after you have supplied your reader with a few convincing arguments, after you have prepared him."

"Yes," the girl agreed, half-lost in thought. "It might sound better."

"See, this is the way you can be useful to me," she added, perking up a little. "When you are constructive."

The professor remained silent.

"Don't you think that destruction should be our last resort?" the girl asked him.

"I don't know," the professor answered. He was looking at the plane trees beyond the parapet.

"It can also bring comfort," he said.

When they walked down the hill, through the park, the sun was already setting behind the trees.

"I am very grateful for your suggestions," the girl

said while trying to keep up with his hurried pace. "Even though I have to rewrite the entire poem."

When they were not talking they could hear the crunch of their steps on the wet gravel.

"You must tell me how I can repay my debt," the girl said.

The professor smiled:

"By forgetting about it," he said.

They had reached the foot of the hill right in front of the rotunda used for outdoor concerts.

"Ha, now I remember what I had forgotten," the girl said.

"What is it?" the professor asked her, stepping over to her left.

"It's about you and the way you've been behaving about that letter."

"What is it?"

"I am not so sure it will please you, but I'm going to tell you anyway," the girl said. "I think you are dominated by one, and only one, feeling: fear."

"Ah!" said the professor.

Every gate of the park had been closed except for the main one, with the long, wrought-iron spikes.

"What do you think?" the girl asked.

"I think you have already paid your debt," the professor answered, slowing down.

155

# XV

At fifty-eight, Mario Cattaneo was an ex-writer. Thirty one years earlier he had published a novel, *Instants,* which had won the "New Writers" Prize, and had been critically acclaimed as "more than promising." Since then, he hadn't written anything else, with the exception of the entry "novel" for a serialized encyclopedia, two articles for a bibliographical journal, which had subsequently failed, and two short essays on the current state of fiction. Struck by sudden sterility, he had never stopped thinking of a future novel, which he would write as soon as he had retired from high school teaching and had cut down on his editorial work. This last activity filled most of his free time: manuscripts of all sizes, some thin, others so thick that they came in cubic boxes like dictionaries, were constantly dropped off by harried messengers with his concierge. He found them there every day, when he went to collect his mail. And there he unwrapped them, weighed them up, and read the name of their authors and their titles; then, back in his study, he lined them all up on a black box seat. When their turn came, he would lie down on his mock-leather couch and start reading them, one by one.

The hope of discovering a *new writer* in a nameless stranger had never abandoned him, even though it had seldom happened in the course of many years. The few times it had occurred, he had experienced an intense and ephemeral sort of happiness, like a quiet but deeply felt sharing in someone else's joy.

More often than not, however, the manuscripts were mediocre and judging them became a mournful task. The most immediate and unequivocal disappointments were caused by novels that did their damnedest to be funny, vainly trusting in the reader's complicity and enthusiastic candor, or in his or her conjugal tolerance and devotion (the all too frequent consequences of comfort and inertia). In those cases, all he could do was soften the punch with the kid gloves of trustworthy reason.

His best intentions were also sorely tested by the so-called memory novels, in which the author tried to "remember everything," probably assuming that was Proust's intent. How to arrest such zeal? Impossible; only the end of the novel seemed to be able to do it, but then again, it was only an interruption, never a conclusion. The problem was that memory novels were inexhaustible and soon exhausted his energies. Then, he would get up from his sofa, pour himself a glass of iced tea, and leaf through the volumes of an endless *Biographical Dictionary*, which had been under publication for the last eighteen years, and was certainly not going to reach the letter Z until after his death. To enter, even if only for a few minutes, into the details of a life diverted and charmed him: the first inklings of a vocation, a nearly fatal fall from a horse, the escape to a new continent, passion at forty-six, an unexpected crime, long-awaited glory, posthumous fame. Whereas memory novels usually ended up erasing time, by reducing it to an endless present of imaginary trepidations, the merest biographical detail ("he died at sunset, the very same day") stirred up in him a swarm of vivid images and intense emotions.

Another work that fascinated him was *Italy During the Hundred Years of the Nineteenth Century (1801-1900)*, day by day, with illustrations, by Comandini, a book that had been mostly derived from newspaper articles. He would open it at random, and read:

> October 31, 1807, Saturday. A certain Mr. Carboni, attorney-at-law, is arrested and detained for several days by the Milan police for having criticized, in the course of a family discussion, the very expensive preparations made in view of Napoleon's imminent arrival.

Or, on the same page, October 16, 1807, Friday.

> Professor Michele Tenon, the curator of the Royal Botanic Gardens in Naples, catches a rare butterfly, seldom spotted in Italy, the *Papilio Mopsa Fabricio*, indigenous to the East Indies.

Or, July 17, 1802, Saturday.

> Near Genova, the gendarmerie discovers six famous brigands hiding in a farm above Acqua Marsa. In the ensuing conflict, the farm is burnt down, a brigand dies in the fire, three are killed, and the remaining two flee.

Or, October 2, 1812, Friday.

Francesco Vaccà-Berlinghieri (1732), the renowned surgeon and writer, dies in Pisa.

These books provided him with a concrete sense of time and change, such as neither the knights of memory nor the fans of the present were able to evoke, admitting they were even aware of it.

Other texts by unknown writers would at times fit within the arbitrary and uncertain, but also fairly precise, scope of publishability. Full of doubts and uneasy interest, he would then read on in the hope of coming across the page that would inevitably make him lean toward a yes or a no. But that seldom occurred, and the doubts lingered on, past the index, and into the hallway, where he was likely to walk his troubles, and where he inevitably met some other member of the family, whether son, wife, or mother-in-law, with whom he would exchange a few platitudes to air his thoughts before returning to his sofa. But he knew that even that did not help, and that the only way to find the words that would allow him both to understand what he felt and to express it was to think for a long time in front of the typewriter.

He had no such problems when it came to authors with known names, belonging to the so-called "stables" of the major publishers: in those instances, his judgment, even though negative, could not change anybody's destiny, nor alter the course of a life (but this no longer bothered him much since nowadays too many, or too few, things could affect a life). The text was inevitably published and what he said on the flaps of the dust jackets would often be the opposite of what he had said in his reports. All it required was to change the adjectives, replace "monotonous" with "enthralling," "anemic" with "vital." "Incongruity" became "fantastic freedom," "mawkishness" "pathos," "arbitrariness" "coherence." "Rigor" and "authenticity" never failed, particularly if in conjunction, and, among the adjectives, one could always resort to "overwhelming": in most (generally the best) cases "not so bad" would have been more appropriate, but "overwhelming" was generally considered more effective. Thus, smoothing corners and filling gaps, transforming false notes into "dissonances," and calling ignorance "reserve," he would write the blurbs of imaginary books that only vaguely corresponded to the real ones. If self-respect kept him from signing them, respect of others did not keep him from writing them. Besides, like most critics and publishers, he could also avail himself of an infinite number of alibis. And in a world in which the *alibi* no longer consisted in *being elsewhere* but rather in *being there*, he remained where he was and justified it with a few more alibis. In the first place there were his financial needs, multiplied by his love life.

Starting with the principle that to maintain a good relationship with one's wife it is necessary to have a mistress, and that to maintain a good relationship with a mistress it is necessary to have yet another one, for the last twelve years he had been the lover of a simultaneous interpreter who, after her initial qualms, had reached an analogous conclusion, at least as far as her own relationship with her husband was concerned. For the last eight years he had also been the lover of one of his colleagues, an exceedingly shy young woman who was utterly unable to bring any discipline into a classroom. During the long conversations that filled the "holes" between one lesson and the next, he had given her bits of advice that had proved useful: to look her students straight in the eye, to talk seriously, to say things that also made sense to her. This last suggestion had particularly struck her, accustomed as she was to teaching as if in a trance, repeating with vehemence and solitary fury strings of words she had learned at the university. He had also advised her against being too tense, at least mentally, and, one afternoon, as they were watching some athletic events on television, in the teachers' lounge, he had drawn her attention to the suppleness of the first runner and the stiffness of the second-to-the-last one. As for the last runner, seen in slow motion, while he was collapsing at the finish line, he looked like the emblem of a desperate and probably deleterious heroism. To get her up to his attic, on a storm-cooled July evening, had been easier than making her understand that her students did not belong to a different species. In fact, it had been very sweet and tender, and he could still remember the two silent, round tears glimmering in her eyes after he had made love to her, just as he had read many years earlier, he no longer knew whether in Maupassant or in D'Annunzio or in both.

To divide his free time between these two women, plus the occasional ones meant to preserve his relationship with his second mistress, required much energy and effort. A few minute precautions had afforded him some breathing space. He had told his wife, for whom so-called "physical" love was a painful test and the expiation of uncommitted sins, that a minor affliction, fortunately not contagious, had temporarily forced him into total abstinence. Much to the relief of both, this had put an end to their love sessions, lugubrious rituals during which, at least for the first few years of their marriage, he had vainly and repeatedly tried to make her understand why she should have rejoiced in his desire, invariably eliciting her tears and stifled sobs. He did not have to make much of an effort to explain to his first mistress how "ugly" things and "beautiful" ones often converged, since she took it upon herself to explain it to him. Endowed with vigorous appetites, she had also shown him how an imperious egoism can often be an exciting erotic ingredient. His second mistress was an odd mixture of the other two women, alternating as she did between lyrical ecstasies and epic orgasms that left him stunned and gratified. But her postcoital shame was a constant disappointment as it deprived him of the most precious pleasure: a sense of complicity. Instead, he had to listen to her questioning the morality of what they did together, and rhapsodizing on the superiority of higher interests over lower ones. At this point, he would generally glance at his watch and discover that it was already very late and that he still had to write two reports for the next day.

Which, anyway, was almost always true. If too much free time could be a problem, as the media maintained, his problem was not having enough time. For the less time he had, the more he took off from his work, so that at the end he would invariably find himself in deep water. In the twenty-three years he had been using this metaphor, not once had he tried to remove its cause. Rather he had justified it in the belief that, far from being threatening to a swimmer, deep water was precisely what he needed, and the deeper the better.

When, in between manuscripts, he happened to leaf through some of the books in his library—the first page of *Moby Dick* or the *Pickwick Papers,* or a passage from *Gulliver's Travels* or *Poil de Carotte*—he would often feel oddly moved, as if these books had been written especially for him by authors from a different planet. What they said spoke to him directly, right there, where he was, standing in his study at that very moment in time: they did not require double takes or second readings to fill him with the invigorating joy of a complete intimacy. But then when he returned to a three-hundred page manuscript in which, by the express will of its author, everything happened, he no longer felt in the right mood to judge it. More often than not an author failed not because he had no good qualities but because he was unable to give anything up. Greedy and childish, he would behave like the clients in a restaurant with an open buffet who gorge themselves on appetizers and are full by the time they get to the entrées, just as the cook had predicted. Occasionally, rereading his reports, he would realize that he had made a mistake in his choice of tone, in his evaluation, in his expectations, and this made him feel terribly responsible. Fortunately, the letters of rejection were written by the editors themselves in accordance with their firm belief that the addressee lacked any objectivity, a belief which the addressees reciprocated quite as firmly. Generous in praises and apologies, like the blurbs and the ads, they strayed far afield into the realm of the imaginary, where truth was seldom met, and then only by accident.

He liked the word "imaginary." The heroine of the novel that he was going to write—as soon as he had gotten rid of all his editorial commitments and was free to devote himself entirely to it—was also a victim of the imaginary: a hysterical pregnancy. He had carefully researched these infrequent occurrences in which the presumed pregnancy continues for the full nine months, often all the way into labor and, at times, even as far as delivery, when, its moment no longer deferrable, truth bursts forth in a sudden and complete release of air. This would be his novel's conclusion and the more he thought about it, the more he found it adhered to all he had understood of the world. When he had told his three women about it, at different times and in different places—in a movie theater, on a staircase, in a cab—all three had expressed some curiosity, as had an editor and two friends, particularly when it came to that finale of sudden deflation and collapse. Judging and correcting other people's texts, he had come to the conclusion that if an idea for a story was really good it would be convincing even when condensed into a few words. And yet, every time he used the wrong noun and adjective while divulging his idea, the entire plot felt weakened, fragile. But that was to be expected: every word is a world, and every slip of the tongue a potential catastrophe. On the other hand, there were also times when he felt that people's interest in his story was mostly elicited by his ability in choosing and placing the right words, the result of long training in rhetoric, and that the moment he started amplifying and expanding it into a novel, his idea would turn out to be a mere bubble, not unlike his heroine's pregnancy. He feared the relentless passage of time and the approach of old age, but found comfort in the thought that most novelists had given their best in their full maturity. However, as the years kept going by, he started running out of examples. DeFoe, Swift, besides a handful of others, were the only classics he was left with.

Cattaneo lived in the oldest part of the city, a fortress of mangy façades pierced by low, dark archways leading into squalid courtyards, with exterior stone stairs and creeping vines, and from these into yet other fenced-in yards, covered with gray plastic skylights, which suddenly opened up into totally new spaces, lined with hardware stores, laundry shops, dusty windows spelling WINE, and all around the steady flapping of the wash drying on the iron railings of the balconies. Here and there, mounds of garbage, pyramids of old tires, and car wrecks piled up right below the boarded-up windows of houses, mostly abandoned except for a few rooms on one or two floors where one could occasionally glimpse an old woman sitting quietly by a stove pipe stuck through the wall.

In one of these courtyards, past two low archways, there was a hillock, and on the hillock there was a one-story home, tucked in the corner of a tall wall behind which soared the buildings of the modern quarter. A wrought-iron arch framed an alley of stone steps leading to the front door. Cattaneo lived here with his family, all still unresigned to this new abode, particularly his wife who, however, had at first shown a faint enthusiasm. But then, the narrowness of the place, its sudden shifts of temperature, both in summer and winter, the shabbiness of the railings on the facing building, all this caused her to turn an envious eye on the modern apartments in the new quarter, and on the cluster of balconies sticking out from what looked like a series of neatly superimposed cubes. With difficulty, Cattaneo had managed to persuade her to wait until he had retired, when he would at last start his novel and a new life. In the meantime, he kept receiving his packages of books and manuscripts in the concierge's apartment smothered in kitchen fumes, and his guests in the only large room of the house, the living room-study, with a sofa bed and windows overlooking a twenty-foot slope.

On that stormy evening, he was enjoying the cool air seated in a large wicker chair on his doorstep. He was looking at the last pinkish clouds drifting above the roofs. That's how the professor found him, with lowered eyelids and arms dangling over the sides of his seat, when he emerged from under the second archway.

"Hello!" he shouted at him as he started climbing the stone steps of the alley.

Cattaneo gave a start, hoisted himself out of his chair, and, readjusting the belt of his trousers over his huge belly, waddled in his direction, and hugged him just a few steps from the front door.

"I was expecting you," he said. "I don't like the way you look."

"I look tired, is that it?'

"Yes," Cattaneo answered, with a worried expression on his face. "What's going on?"

"I'm going to tell you," the professor said, climbing the last few steps and preceding him to the door. "That's precisely why I have come to see you."

He walked into the hallway and, noticing the piles of books, asked:

"Your wife's not around?"

"No, she's at the seaside," Cattaneo answered switching on the light. "Don't you see how calm I am?"

"What about Carla?"

"She's also at the seaside," Cattaneo said, letting him enter the living room ahead of him.

"Pia's gone too?" the professor asked him, as he

167

walked into a large room randomly partitioned by bookcases.

"No, she's still around," Cattaneo answered. He had made him sit next to him, on a low sofa, opposite the window.

"How do you find the time to write?" the professor asked him.

"I don't."

"Aren't you tired of this kind of life?"

"Very," Cattaneo answered, lowering his eyes.

"But you're not going to give it up?"

"No," Cattaneo answered, rolling his head, which he had rested on the back of the sofa, in his friend's direction. "Why do you ask?"

"Because you're spreading yourself too thin," the professor answered, touching his glasses.

"If anything I should cut down on my daily work. Not the rest."

"What about your novel?"

"I'll write it, don't worry."

He looked at him:

"I know you no longer believe me, but it doesn't matter." The professor remained silent.

"I am an underground man," Cattaneo added. "I am accumulating tensions for the day I'll start writing."

"Could it be that, somehow, this sort of life suits you better than some other one?"

Cattaneo looked at him with surprise:

"No, I don't think so."

"How can you say that?"

"Because I'm not happy with it."

"Still, for you this may be the least of all evils."

Cattaneo shook his head.

"No, I don't think so."

"I'm saying this because I'm beginning to realize

how easy it is to fool oneself," the professor went on, "particularly when it comes to what we want."

Without looking at him, Cattaneo asked:

"Has something happened to you?"

"Yes," the professor answered. He rested his hand on his black-leather briefcase. "I've been attacked in a magazine."

"By whom?"

"I don't know."

"Is it important?"

"Not in itself, but it is very important to me," the professor answered. "And that is my problem."

Cattaneo pointed to a small liquor cabinet under a collection of classics:

"Would you like something to drink?"

"No, thank you."

"Do you mind if I do?"

He grabbed a bottle of whisky and a glass. The professor waited until he had swallowed the first sip, then, with an altered tone of voice, asked:

"Do you feel like listening to me?"

"Of course I do," Cattaneo answered, and returned to sit next to him. "But don't get all upset."

The professor raised his voice:

"I am calm! And that is why I can ask you, quite calmly, to listen to me."

"Hear, hear," Cattaneo said, watching him. "I would have never thought you could be so emotional."

"Why?"

"If anything, you are a maniac," Cattaneo continued. "Yes, you suffer from fixations. But never to the point of being blocked by them. You've always been able to pursue your interests."

"That's no longer true. Now I am unable to concentrate on my work."

"This is odd," Cattaneo said. "Just because of an article?"

"Yes, I am not like you."

Cattaneo looked at him questioningly.

"Yes. I am not used to dodging problems, or to putting them off," the professor continued. "I like to get to the bottom of things."

"And what do you find at the bottom?"

"Generally what I am looking for, which is why I cannot accept what's going on now."

Cattaneo asked him:

"And that's where we differ?"

"Yes. Your character is completely different. Forgive me for telling you so but you are not used to facing up to things, not if you can help it."

"Oh."

"All you have to do is have a look at your private life," the professor went on, "at the way in which you organize, or rather, don't organize your work."

"Well, that's a long story."

"Of course."

"Are you here to attack me or to tell me about yourself?" Cattaneo asked him.

"To tell you about myself."

"Then tell me."

The professor collected his thoughts for a while, sighed, and then said:

"I would like two things from you: first of all I would like you to tell me what you think of the letter, and then I would like you to read my answer."

He tried to open the briefcase he held on his knees but did not succeed. He pressed the metal clasp twice without being able to release the spring. Then he tried to yank it open but Cattaneo intervened.

"Give it here," he said.

He gently pressed the metal plate, then pushed it downward to let it spring open. He handed the briefcase back to the professor who muttered:

"I can't even open a briefcase any more."

He pulled out *The Voice of Antiquity*, already folded over to the page with the letter. Cattaneo glanced at the title and then started reading. Halfway through, he smiled, turned to the professor and said: ,

"He sure doesn't pull any punches, does he?"

The professor kept staring at him tensely, controlling his breathing. Cattaneo looked up at the darkness beyond the window, emptied his glass, put it back on the table, and, pursing his lips, went on reading. At the end, he looked pensive, his eyes wandering aimlessly above the books.

"So?" the professor asked him.

"It isn't easy."

"I know, but what do you make of it?"

"It's full of hatred."

"Yes, that's what everybody says."

Cattaneo nodded in silence, and let his head rest against the back of the sofa. The professor went on:

"I sort of thought that, with your experience in reading manuscripts, you would immediately get an idea of who could have written it."

Flattered, if somewhat embarrassed, Cattaneo picked up the magazine and said:

"Let's see."

He cupped his chin in the palm of his right hand and concentrated on the letter. After a long pause, he said:

"In the first place, this is someone who is used to answering his own questions. In other words, he is a teacher."

"I agree."

"All this is further evidenced by the procedural, I'd even say gestural, tone," Cattaneo said, his eyes searching the letter for a concrete example. "Here it is: 'no problem so far,'" and he accompanied the words with a sweeping gesture.

"I agree."

"In the second place, he is a contemporary of yours," Cattaneo continued. "As indicated by the 'alas' with which he refers to remote university years. Young people only bemoan the present."

"You are right."

"Thirdly, and you can deduce this from both his premises and his punctiliousness, he is a moralist unhappy with himself and the rest of the world, that is to say, chock-full of repressed aggressiveness. He is a time bomb that's always exploding at the wrong time."

Perplexed, the professor knitted his brow.

"Besides, you know what's the weirdest thing?" Cattaneo continued. "His language. So defensive."

Expecting a question, he turned toward the professor, but the professor remained silent. So he went on:

"Do you know what I mean by 'defensive'? A language that would like to attack but is afraid of the risks involved."

More puzzled than convinced, the professor kept on listening.

"He is a linguistic pervert, you see?"

A long pause followed. Cattaneo was again concentrating on the letter. All of a sudden, he raised his eyes, as if struck by an unexpected intuition.

"Now I understand," he said with cold enthusiasm. "He is a maniac."

"What sort of maniac?"

"Sexual. He suffers from sexual obsessions."

172

The professor shrugged his shoulders and spread his arms out:

"So what's new? Don't we all?"

"True, but his are very particular. Let me show you."

He went to the bookcase next to the window and pulled out a book with no jacket and hardly any binding.

"I found it in a bookstall, a few evenings ago," Cattaneo said. "It is a nineteenth-century book, somewhat rickety in its conclusions but with a few interesting cases. Here, read this."

He handed him the book opened to page 38.

The professor read: "The case of Count B.H.":

Count B.H., from Wiesbaden, was used to paying a monthly visit to a notorious lady of pleasure, during which visit, maintaining the strictest of silences, he would cut a lock of her tresses. This act proving sufficient in slaking his desires, he would then pay the hussy and silently take his leave.

"What does this have to do with the letter?" the professor asked after reading the passage.

"You don't have a single friend who fits that description?" asked Cattaneo, who had watched him attentively throughout the reading.

"Not that I know of," the professor answered, taking off his glasses. "As usual, you are digressing. All this is completely off the mark."

"Not as much as it may seem," Cattaneo said, sitting down. "You can't even imagine what a complex nexus there is between this sort of twisted behavior and language."

"Oh, I do, I do. But it is difficult to unravel," the professor retorted. "You've shifted the whole question onto the level that interests you most, but I don't want to delve into it. I want to get out of it, and find a plausible hypothesis for my situation."

Cattaneo leaned back and looked straight ahead.

"You might be right, this is probably not the easiest approach," he said.

He thought for a while and then added:

"Anyway, I didn't mean someone who only behaves in that particular way, but anyone with a compulsive personality and a tendency to obsess. It can manifest itself in a number of ways, but the origin is always the same. Don't you know anyone with that sort of problem?"

The professor shrugged his shoulders:

"Of course."

"Who?"

"I don't see how it could help."

"Oh, it can. I'm sure of it."

The professor stroked his chin with his right hand.

"If that's the case, I know more than one."

"Give me one example," Cattaneo insisted, as he poured himself another glass of whisky.

"Bini, for instance. In the course of his lectures he always resorts to erotic examples. Never fails. Even in the most abstruse instances, he always pulls it off."

"How do you know?"

"His students told me. But he holds a chair in paleography and diplomacy. I doubt he is much interested in my field."

"Give me another example," said Cattaneo. "Think of someone else."

"Rivoli," the professor answered with an engrossed look on his face. "He's a know-it-all. Do you remember, back in school, there was always a kid who was a know-it-all? Well, at fifty-two, Rivoli is still that kid."

"Some people believe I am too," Cattaneo smiled.

The professor looked at him nonplussed:

"Who does? One of your women?"

"Yes."

"I'm not surprised. I hope you don't take them seriously. They say it because they are in love, or to flatter you, but they don't believe it for a second."

"No, that's not exactly correct, but it doesn't matter," Cattaneo said. "Tell me about Rivoli."

"His ideal is to know what nobody else knows," the professor answered, making himself more comfortable. "To have read all the books before they have even been written, which, on occasion, he has been able to do thanks to his connections and a few indiscretions. And what's more, he has another suicidal obsession—he expects to remember everything."

"That's not another obsession," Cattaneo said. "It's the same thing."

"Maybe," the professor answered. "All I know is that his students hold their breath every time he tries to remember some citation. If he can't, his voice cracks."

"How do you relate to him?"

"Horribly. We pretend we don't see each other."

Cattaneo shook his head.

"In that case, he's not the one. Think of somebody else."

The professor thought it over, hesitated, and then said:

"Of course, there is always Daverio, but I don't think he's the one."

"Who is this Daverio?"

"He's a colleague who used to court my wife."

Cattaneo turned toward him with a look that expressed at once surprise and pleasure:

"Ah! That's all?"

And, since the professor did not answer, Cattaneo asked him:

"Before or after you got married?"

"Before and after," the professor said, folding his arms.

"And it doesn't bother you?"

"Not much," the professor answered with calm. "She doesn't really care."

"If I were you I wouldn't be so sure. Besides, obviously he does."

"That might well be true."

"Does he have a tendency to obsess about things?"

"Yes."

"Give me an example," Cattaneo said, changing his position on the sofa.

"He has a thing for new books. He always buys two copies, one to read and the other to put away in his bookcases, so it doesn't get damaged."

"How much does he spend?"

"A fortune. So much that he's ashamed to tell even his wife. He will tour a dozen bookstores to find the perfect copy."

"From what you're telling me, he may well be the writer of that letter," Cattaneo said, glancing at his dirty books on their shabby wooden shelves. "Does he have other obsessions?"

"Yes, he does, but this one is boundless," the professor answered. "For instance, he cannot stand to hear a book open with a crack," and he pretended to crack a book open on his knees. "Once, to find the perfect copy of a book that he had heard was almost out of print, he scoured the entire city like a soul in torment, and when he finally found it, he bought three copies. But none of them was perfect, so he had them bound anyway.''

"Who told you all this?''

"My wife. They spend hours on the phone.''

Cattaneo looked perplexed.

"It's a strange relationship, don't you think?''

"Yes, but I'd rather not talk about it,'' the professor answered. Then, with a visible effort, he went on:

"Every page must be perfectly smooth, without a single crease, unless, of course, the paper is glossy.''

"Glossy? Why?''

"Because in that case, a good iron and a drop of water will do the trick. There will only be a little sign left, and so neat that, according to him, it couldn't possibly compromise the book, quite the contrary, it might even lend it a personal touch.''

Cattaneo was more and more surprised:

"Where did he come up with all these rules?''

"Like most maniacs, he has imposed them upon himself: the iron laws of a perfect universe where each transgression must be punished and expiated. When he tours the city in search of the perfect copy, he is at once indulging and expiating his vice.''

"Why do you think he is doing all this?''

"I don't know.''

Then he added:

"Unless, of course, you still believe in the answers of psychology.''

"He has another big obsession,'' he went on. "His hair.''

"Why, he has a lot?''

"No, very little,'' the professor answered, glancing

at Cattaneo's thick, wiry mane. "And that's his problem. For the last twenty years he has tried everything: lotions with placenta, tar, petroleum, electric treatments, he has even resorted to acupuncture. Now he is trying herbs."

"I would keep my eye on him," Cattaneo said.

The professor looked perplexed:

"Others have said the same thing."

"So?"

"Somehow it seems too easy, too banal," the professor answered, putting his briefcase on the floor. "It would be the same old story."

"But it is always the same old story."

"Somehow, I feel it is a worse enemy than Daverio."

"Never trust your feelings," Cattaneo said. "They are generally wrong anyway."

The professor was observing him:

"So, according to you, what should I do?"

"Try to draw him into the open. Provoke him," Cattaneo answered. "Sound him out."

He lowered his eyes.

"Use your wife, if necessary."

"No, never."

"Listen to me," Cattaneo said, looking up at him. "I'm not proposing anything ugly, don't worry. Just a more light-handed approach."

"No, I don't like that sort of tack," the professor said. "I can't accept it."

"Then just close your eyes!" Cattaneo exclaimed. "As you've always done. You always close your eyes."

The professor looked at him dumbfounded.

"You know I'm right," Cattaneo insisted. "You've always preferred to concentrate on the symptoms rather than on the disease. But here, it is the entire organism that's sick, rotten."

178

"You are raving," the professor exclaimed, somewhat flustered.

"Not at all," Cattaneo retorted. "If you really want to get to the bottom of this matter, as you claim you do, then you have to start with yourself and your wife."

"With myself and my wife?"

"Yes, what's so strange about it?"

The professor, who in the meantime had straightened himself up in his seat, hesitated a while and then sighed.

"You are digressing again," he said, disappointed but also somewhat reassured. "Let's try to stick to the subject."

"But this is the subject," Cattaneo insisted. "The way you react, and all that it implies. One mere enemy can't be enough to push you over the edge."

He poured some more whisky into his glass, took a sip, and added:

"What I mean is that if he has gotten to you it's because you were already weak."

"Where am I weak?" the professor asked.

Cattaneo stared at him with renewed curiosity.

"I don't know," he answered. "Maybe in your life, your marriage, your work, your aspirations, all your alibis. If you have reached the age of reckonings, the problem with you is that you always make them square. You're a real master at that. But obviously something doesn't really fit, something crucial, and he has realized it."

The professor swallowed.

"You should talk."

"Indeed," Cattaneo nodded.

Then, pointing to the briefcase on the floor, with an altered tone of voice, he asked:

179

"In the meantime, why don't you show me your answer."

When the professor pulled out a sheet of paper full of erasures, Cattaneo craned his neck toward it and asked:

"Can't I read it myself?"

"No, you wouldn't understand a thing," the professor answered. "And, please, don't pay too much attention to the details. This is only a first draft."

"All right."

"I'm sure there are quite a few problems," the professor added.

"Please, stop wasting our time with preambles. Read."

The professor looked at the paper in his hand, coughed, and, instead of reading, said:

"At the beginning I would like to point out the fact that to write an anonymous letter is a pusillanimous act, though I could use another adjective such as vile, or maybe infamous would be more appropriate, or sordid. What do you think?"

Cattaneo shook his head.

"I think it would be a big mistake to start your letter on that sort of note," he answered. "How could you even consider such an absurd beginning?"

"Because that's what I think."

"And you also think that's enough of a reason? What do you want, to destroy your enemy or to write a confession?"

"To destroy my enemy."

"Very good!" Cattaneo exclaimed. "In that case the first thing to keep in mind," and he stuck out the thumb of his right hand, "is the audience, the focus of all rhetoric. Who is it you are addressing?"

180

"Him."

"Not the readers?"

"Both."

"All right, that's already better," Cattaneo said. "According to you, who was he addressing?"

The professor thought about it for a while.

"First of all, me."

"I tend to agree," Cattaneo said. "He wanted to hit you because you were his mark, and he used the others as mere witnesses. But your case is different. You don't want to hit him, you don't even know who he is. Rather, you want to persuade others of his wrongdoing."

"True!" the professor exclaimed, pulling a pen from his pocket.

"In that case you must use the most effective tone," Cattaneo said. "A tone of absolute detachment. Detachment is always very convincing, and never comical."

"What if I don't feel detached?"

"Pretend you are," Cattaneo answered. "Invent your detachment. Imagine that you are coaching me in something that doesn't concern you in the least."

"What should I tell you?"

Cattaneo smoothed the hair on his temples.

"Say that the attention your anonymous attacker has devoted to you is both flattering and undeserved."

"That's a little too much."

"Yes, I think so too," Cattaneo agreed pensively. "Still, we should try to follow the principle of dynamics: 'To each action the same and opposite reaction.'"

The professor muttered:

"Fine but I really don't see what that has to do with this."

"If you sound too detached, or too ironic, people might suspect you are the opposite."

"So how should I sound?"

Stretching his hand toward the sheet of paper, Cattaneo made an erasing gesture:

"Get rid of 'flattering,' but keep 'attention.' You must express your astonishment at having received so much attention in a magazine article. No," he interrupted himself. "No, this won't work with the readers."

The professor crossed out two lines and then said:

"What if I started as follows: 'It is with great astonishment. . . '"

"Yes!" Cattaneo exclaimed. "On the other hand, what is it that astonishes you?"

"So much attention seems a little out of proportion with the rather specialized linguistic nature of the subject."

Cattaneo nodded.

"Yes, 'a little' works well."

The professor underlined 'a little' with his pen.

"Then I should say that I am rather baffled by the vehemence of my anonymous censor. . ."

"No," Cattaneo interrupted him. "Too much psychology. Do you really think your audience cares about your reactions? You should worry about their reactions."

"Couldn't they coincide with mine?"

"No, that only happens by accident in a few fortunate cases."

Then he added:

"And yours is clearly not one of them."

The professor, pen in hand, waited. Cattaneo went on:

"You could say that such vehemence seems somewhat peculiar and then immediately move on to the next point."

Raising his hand, as if to defend himself, the professor asked:

"Couldn't I hint at the fact that such vehemence might be explained by 'vague personal reasons'?"

"Absolutely not!" Cattaneo exclaimed. "You should not worry about the writer's reasons or otherwise your readers will become suspicious."

"I see," the professor said. Then, he glanced at the paper, hesitated, and, tentatively, went on:

"Here I would like to mention his useless display of scholarship, his inane claims to erudition."

Cattaneo hid his face in both his hands and then let them slide slowly down his cheeks.

"Please excuse my saying so, but you don't even know where to start. Expressions such as 'display of scholarship,' and 'erudition' are only good for autodidacts who like to criticize official culture. But you are part of that official culture, aren't you?"

The professor crossed out a line while Cattaneo went on:

"As for the adjective 'useless,' I'd advise you to take it easy. Is what he says right or not?"

The professor shrugged.

"I can't possibly answer your question with a 'yes' or a 'no,'" he said.

"But that is the only answer your audience wants. Is it true or not that your etymology of 'hypocrite' was incomplete?"

"It is true," the professor answered. "But that was neither the right place nor the best time to get into it."

"I'm sorry but I don't agree with you," Cattaneo said. "Anyway, you'd better not admit it. Rather, you should say that what mattered to you most was to focus on the last meaning, that is to say, on 'dissembler.' And that you deliberately left out the rest as minutiae for specialists."

The professor started writing, muttering a few words as he went:

"The last meaning . . . dissembler . . . minutiae for specialists."

"No, not 'for specialists,'" Cattaneo intervened. "Better say 'inessential.'"

The professor struck out 'minutiae for specialists' and wrote:

"'Inessential minutiae.'"

Then, he looked up and said:

"Now we must move on to the third point. Are you tired?"

"No," Cattaneo, who had momentarily closed his eyes, answered. "Go on."

"So," the professor started with a sigh. "At this point, I would like to say, in one way or another, possibly with some detachment. . . anyway, the basic idea is this: he's the 'whited sepulcher,' if anybody is."

Cattaneo poured some more whisky into his glass, drank it in silence while the professor watched him, and then said:

"It's childish."

Then, he added:

"Please, give me that paper, I'm sure I'll be able to read it."

The professor complied.

Cattaneo read it through, then he leaned his head against the back of the sofa and said:

"This is totally off the mark. It's drab, opaque, pedantic. It lacks imagination."

"It's all wrong?"

"What you need is hatred! A hatred so lucid as to

sound like detachment! I remember the beginning of an argument some philologists were having. One of them said: 'Have you ever seen a dung beetle emerge from a drain and start writing?' "

"You call that detachment?"

"Yes, because he was able to create an image! You don't create anything. Do you see what I mean?"

As he was saying this, he got up and went to the window framed by vine leaves still dripping from the storm. He opened it and a draft of fresh air immediately swept through the room.

"Ah!" Cattaneo exclaimed, breathing in deeply.

"Imagination?" the professor muttered at his back. "Easy to say."

"No! It should not be too easy to say," Cattaneo said.

He leaned on the windowsill, then turned around.

"Anyway, you get the idea of what tone you should use?"

"Vaguely."

"Come, you need some fresh air, it will clear up your head," Cattaneo told him.

The professor leaned on the windowsill next to him.

They could hear the sound of a man's steps approaching through the dimly lit archway that led into the courtyard.

"You must think of a particular person, someone who hates you," Cattaneo said. "You'll see, it will help you."

The professor nodded, looking at the darkening sky.

"Even if it is not Daverio," Cattaneo added, "think of him."

# XVI

Naked and steaming, hot water dripping down his face, Daverio stood in the tub waiting, with limp patience, for the accomplishment of a special event: for the lather of his shampoo to cease crackling and gradually dry on his scalp. Finally he turned the shower on: under the downpour, he opened his mouth and kept the upper part of his body bent forward, huddling over on himself. Groping about while the water kept splashing on his face, he managed to turn the shower off, and then stood up straight, arms akimbo, eyes fixed on the misty surface of the mirror. He raised his right leg and let it drip into the tub. Slowly shifting the weight of his body beyond the edge of the tub, he placed his right foot on the bathmat and, standing on it, raised his left leg over the tub. When he brought both feet together, he caught a blurred glimpse of himself in the mirror and immediately remembered the stuffed flamingo he had seen years earlier at the Museum of Natural History. He started shivering. With chattering teeth, he grabbed his bath-robe and clumsily managed to get it on. Then he started rubbing his arms, alternating from one to the other. Having thus reactivated his circulation, he dragged the mat in front of the mirror with his feet and, bending forward, brought his head toward the glass. The long fluorescent bulb, encased in an opaque plastic sheath, cast its bleak light on the skin he uncovered by parting his hair with his fingertips. Having thus exposed a central area he thrust his head still closer to the mirror and, raising his eyes, peered at it, not without some difficulty. He drew his head back for a minute and then again brought it close to the mirror. He ran a wide-toothed comb through his hair, which he then flattened down by pressing a towel on the crown of his head. When he thought he had achieved his purpose, he removed the towel and watched his hair slowly lift. He examined it long and hard, then he looked at his bloodshot eyes and their puffy lids.

"Are you there?" he called out.

Comb in hand, he waited for an answer but only heard the hiss of the trolley bus in the street below. He opened the bathroom door and leaned out into the hallway.

"Are you there? Please answer."

From the bedroom, she asked him:

"What do you want?"

"Would you please come here a second?"

He heard her get out of bed and step into her slippers. Then he drew back into the bathroom, wrapped his robe tightly around himself, and, sitting on the edge of the tub, waited for her. When she opened the door and started making her way through the steam, he told her:

188

"Listen to me."

"Tell me."

"I know you can be objective. I'm counting on it, so, please, be as objective as you can."

"All right, I will."

"Look," he said.

He dropped his head and pushed it forward, as if offering it to the guillotine. Standing perfectly straight, she asked him:

"Is it about your hair again?"

"Yes," he answered, without changing his posture. "Check it out."

She brought her face a few inches closer.

"How does it look?" he asked her.

"Exactly as it looked the last time," she answered, grazing it with her fingers and spreading it apart in one spot.

"Don't touch it!" he yelled, still keeping his head bent. She pulled back.

"I'm sorry," he added. "Have another look."

"But I have already told you, it's exactly as it was last time."

"Really?"

She had again bent over his head, though not quite as close as before, and examined it.

"Yes."

"This means that the herb treatment is working," he said, raising his head.

"That I can't tell you," she answered, walking back to the door. "I don't trust herbs as much as you do. In any case, you don't seem to have lost any since last time."

"I thank you," he said. "May I ask you one more thing, later?"

"About your hair?"

"Yes, after I have rubbed the lotion in."

"All right," she said, clutching the door handle.

Then, staring at him, she added:

"What you really need is to get your head examined, forget your hair."

"I know, I know," he answered, walking toward the door.

When, ten minutes later, he called out to her again, she answered from the kitchen:

"No, it's too hot in there, you come here."

So, he rewrapped himself in his robe and, taking a last look at his head in the mirror, quickly ran his comb through his hair a couple of times; then he cast a furtive glance at the comb holding it up against the light, put it back on the shelf, and left the bathroom.

She was waiting for him, standing with her back against the cupboard. He placed a chair in front of her, and sat on it.

"Please have another look," he told her.

"At what?"

"At my hair. You haven't yet seen it after the lotion. The effect is quite different. Besides, I want to know how it compares with the way it looked a while ago."

She bent over his head:

"What do you want to know?"

"Is there more or less from when I first started using the herb lotion?"

She clasped his head with her two hands and examined it from above while slowly tilting it, first to the right, then to the left, and, finally, downward.

"Certainly not more," she answered. "What do you expect?"

Daverio kept his head stiffly bowed:

"Why do you say that?"

190

"Because at your age the hair you lose no longer grows back."

Without moving an inch, Daverio asked her:

"Are you saying this because it is a theory of yours or because you have just ascertained it."

"For both reasons."

Daverio stood up from his chair and opened the refrigerator. Pouring himself a glass of mineral water, he said:

"Forget your theories, since I don't think the way you think. What I am interested in is the truth."

He emptied his glass, walked back to her, sat down again on his chair, and offered her his head.

"In fact, the truth is the last thing you want to hear."

"That's not true."

"Do you want me to tell you that you have more hair? If you want me to, I will."

Without answering, Daverio craned his neck still further toward her. She bent over his head again for a minute and then exclaimed:

"I'm sorry, but if you really want the truth, it's thinner!"

"Look again."

"Yes, it is thinner, no need to close one's eyes to it, it is thinner. Right here!" and, with the tip of her nail, she touched a spot on the right side. "I remember very clearly that here the white of the scalp did not show quite as much."

"Anywhere else?"

"Yes, on the other side as well. Just a touch."

"You mean, compared to the last time you looked at it?" he asked, thrusting his head yet closer.

"How can I say for sure? It is thinner compared to some time ago."

191

"You're sure?"

"Yes."

With a deep sigh, Daverio raised his head. The mere effort of keeping it bowed that long had again reddened his eyes.

"You really think so?"

"Yes."

He closed his eyes, wrapped his robe tighter around himself, and remained motionless.

She asked him:

"What are you doing?"

Daverio spread out his arms. Keeping his eyes shut, he asked:

"Could it be because you are seeing it wet?"

"No. I always check it when it's wet."

"And, keeping in mind that when it is wet it always looks thinner, you still notice a difference?"

"Yes."

Daverio reopened his eyes.

"So be it," he nodded.

He was looking outside the window at the poplars by the racetrack.

"Please, don't look that way," she pleaded.

"All right."

He stood up.

"Anyway, it looks thinner compared to how long ago?"

"I don't know," she said. "Two or three years."

"Two," Daverio asked, "or three?"

"I don't really know. Maybe three."

Then, stealing a look at him, she added:

"Maybe even four."

"That changes everything!" Daverio exclaimed. "If it is thinner compared to four or five years ago, then that's hardly news. Are you sure?"

"Yes."

"Swear it."

"You know I don't like to swear to such nonsense."

"Then give me your word of honor."

"You have it, but about what?"

"About the fact that it is thinner compared to five years ago."

"Actually I said four years ago," she answered, following him with her eyes. "Besides, how can I possibly be sure of the exact date?"

"But you are at least sure of your perception."

"Yes, yes, however vague that was."

"Word of honor?"

"I've already said so. You have my word."

Daverio brushed his wet hair with his fingertips.

"Without considering the fact that back then you weren't nearly as thorough in your examinations," he added. "Which means that, in reality, all these differences might not even be there."

She glanced at him without saying a word.

"What do you think?"

"I don't know."

"But you can't exclude the possibility."

"No, I can't."

Daverio let out a short sigh. He had approached the window and had leaned his hands against the panes.

"Is that it?" she asked him.

"Yes," Daverio answered letting his arms hang limply at his sides.


Shortly afterwards, in the bedroom, Daverio dropped his robe on a chair and, stark naked, tiptoed to the wardrobe with the full-length on the front of it. She was lying on the bed, staring at the ceiling.

"I wanted to ask you something," he said. "But please don't act surprised."

He had pulled a shirt out of the second drawer.

"What is it?"

"Something quite unimportant," Daverio answered, unbuttoning the shirt. "Just try to imagine you are another woman."

"Who?"

"Nobody. She doesn't exist and has nothing to do with me. This is just an imaginary case," Daverio answered, slipping into his shirt.

"A woman who is in love with her husband," he continued, "and doesn't know that he is having an affair."

"O.K."

"There is also another man who is in love with her, but as long as things are the way they are he has no chance of taking her away from her husband."

"Of course not."

"Why not?" Daverio asked, opening the third drawer.

"I'm trying to follow your line of thinking," she answered. "Obviously, as long as she is in love with her husband the other man doesn't have much of a chance."

"Granted, but are you saying that he never will?"

"How can I know," she answered, turning on her side. "That is often the case."

"True, but one can never know beforehand," Daverio said, looking at her in the mirror. "It might be just a matter of waiting."

"For what?'

"For the right moment."

"If it ever comes," she answered.

"But it cannot be ruled out that it might."

"You go on living without ever ruling out anything," she said, resuming her earlier position. "But sooner or later, life does it for you."

"I was only talking of a hypothetical situation."

"So?" she said, staring at the chandelier. "What I said is also valid for your hypothetical situation."

Turning his back to her, Daverio sat on the edge of the bed and started putting his clothes on.

"Anyway, we have digressed from my imaginary case," he said. "Now, about that hypothetical character, what should he do?"

"He should wait, I don't see what else he could do."

"Granted, but in the meantime? Should he tell her that her husband is having an affair?"

"No, never."

"Why?"

"Because it would be an unforgivable mistake. How can you fail to see that?"

Daverio had opened the fourth drawer.

"But is it right to let her believe in a love that is no longer there?"

"Why, you would tell her in the name of justice?"

"Not me," Daverio answered. "The other man."

"All right, the other man, as you wish. Don't you think she would see through his motives?"

Daverio closed the drawer.

"In that case, he will never be able to tell her," he said.

She turned back on her side and slipped an arm under the pillow.

"He could write an anonymous letter."

Daverio turned toward her:

"I don't think he would ever do that."

After a pause, he asked her:

"And if she discovered it on her own, what chance would he have to win her over, afterwards?"

"Not much."

"What do you mean 'not much'?"

"If he had much of a chance, he would have already succeeded."

Daverio remained perfectly still.

"What about the husband?"

"Oh, the husband," she answered shrugging her shoulders.

"I think the husband is the key character. He is the one who has to be eliminated."

"It's incredible how little you understand about these matters," she said, staring at the door.

Daverio nodded:

"Possibly."

After a while, he said:

"Can you still put up with me?"

"I don't know."

"You know you are free to do what you want."

"Yes, I know. We are all free, but we only do what we can."

Daverio walked to the bed and sat next to her.

"Just a few minutes ago I was asking a bunch of absurd questions, wasn't I?" he said, taking her left hand in his. She left it there, inert.

"I'm exhausted," he added. "But one day this period will be over."

"You have always been exhausted," she said.

"No, this time I really don't know how it's going to end," Daverio said, bowing his head.

She pulled her hand away.

"What do you mean?"

"Nothing."

"Now you even expect me to comfort you," she told him, propping herself up on her elbows.

"No," Daverio said. "All this hurts you, doesn't it?"

"Why do you ask?"

"Answer me."

"Yes."

Daverio stroked her hand for a long time, then softly he said:

"This is no good."

"What do you expect?" she asked him. "At times I wonder whether you are just childish or really sick."

"You shouldn't be the one to suffer," Daverio muttered.

He bent over her and lightly touched her shoulder. Then he turned his glimmering eyes toward the hallway:

"It won't last long."

Six hours later, hidden among the piles of books on his desk, under the quartz chandelier and in front of the radio with the fluorescent clock, Daverio pulled Reinach's *Mithridates Agrimony* out of its leather case and a tiny key, hidden along its spine, fell onto the glass of his desktop. He opened the middle drawer and pulled out his diary. He started to write:

> Seen her two hours ago. I only speak of one thing, she of everything else. No progress. On the contrary, involution (on my part, of course). To depend is terrible. He, off on a wild goose chase to Santa Margherita. She, oddly absent-minded, worried about other things. Never about me. I don't know how much longer it can last. Freedom to choose—forced choices. I often think of

a solution, as usual in moments of crisis. But this time more seriously, more calmly.

He raised his head and, with lowered lids and a weary face, stared at the clock for a long time. Then, he reread what he had written. Carefully, with a felt-tipped pen, he started striking out some of the letters, so that no one could recognize them and decipher the words. When he was done, he reread the whole thing, as if he had just come across it:

> See    two hours ago. I only speak of one thing, he of everything else. No progress. On the contrary, involution (on my part, of course). To pend is terrible.    off on a wild goose chase to    anta    gheri .    oddly absent    rie, about other things. Never about me. I don't know how much longer it can last. Freedom to choose-forced choices. I often think of a    ion, as usual in moments of    is. But this time more seriously, more calmly.

Then he wrote:

Exhaustion:
1. To resume the *Epatos* treatment.
2. Read two pages of the *History of Technology* every day.
3. Always walk from home to school and back.
4. Don't think of her.

He erased the last two words.

Underneath, he drew a circle and, within the circle, a diameter. Then he drew another diameter perpendicular to the first one. Then two diagonals passing through the center. Then a series of lines, both horizontal and vertical, until the circle was perfectly enclosed within a square.

Then he got up and went to the window. He leaned his hot forehead against the pane. A few boys were playing ball in the circle of light cast by a lamp hanging from a wire stretched between two houses. Every time the ball flew up in the air, he could see only their faces, as if they no longer had bodies, and the light lifted them up and brought them closer to his window. As a boy, he had played in that same street, and even now he was alive just as they were, he and they were still alive, and he could imagine himself down in the street, playing. The street, beyond his tears, glittered and wavered. Finally, he was able to cry, with a long, low moan, until he heard his wife's steps in the hallway. Then he tried to control himself, his face still pressed against the windowpane, and gradually he calmed down.

# XVII

In the rosy, tender twilight of a summer evening, the professor rang the gate bell of a small villa that stood in the center of a tiny park on the outskirts of the city. A covered alley flanked by dwarf shrubs led to a raised porch. Here the professor, hands clasped behind his back and eyes scanning the zodiac that decorated the vaulted ceiling, waited in vain for the door to open. Then he pressed another bell, hidden in the mouth of a lion.

"Oh, it's you, professor," the maid murmured, bending her head toward her right shoulder. "I'm sorry, I thought someone else had gotten the door."

"Am I early?"

"No, no. Professor Salutati is already here," the maid answered, letting him walk ahead on the red carpet and closing the door behind him. "But, as you probably already know, my lady will be a little late. She asks you to please excuse her and make yourself at home."

The professor left his hat in her hands and she hung it on a peg of the coatrack. Walking in front of the huge, gold-framed mirror that covered the left wall, the professor cast a sidelong glance at his portly figure and instinctively sucked in his belly under the vest. In front of him, a staircase led to a balcony that curved above his head. He automatically lifted his eyes and saw Salutati, elbows resting on the banister and chin cupped in his hands, who greeted him:

"I will be right with you, my dear."

He straightened himself up.

"I've come up here to admire these splendid nautical charts," and he pointed over his shoulder at two Renaissance planispheres that covered the entire wall. Then he walked along the balcony and, slowly, climbed down the stairs, grazing the banister with his right hand.

"I am delighted to see you," he said, walking toward him with open arms. "But what is that somber look on your face?"

He hugged him, giving him a light pat on his shoulder.

"Ever so worried," he added. "And ineffable. You are never there."

"Where?"

"On campus, of course," Salutati answered and went ahead of him into a large, resplendent hall. "In any case, all is well with you, I hope?"

He sat in front of a majolica fireplace covered by a hood that flared down from the center of the ceiling like an immense inverted funnel.

"Sit here," he invited him, cuddling up in the corner of the sofa. "Tell me about yourself. What have you been up to? Why aren't you happy?"

"Why, are you?"

"Me?" Salutati answered. "But, my dear, when have I ever been happy. You know me, I am a restless soul. But you, you have always been a strong man, strong and confident. I have always envied you."

"Is that so?"

"Yes," Salutati assented. "Sincerely, to use that obnoxious adverb."

The professor tried to smile with detachment.

"You have always believed in your work," Salutati went on, "and in that unspeakable thing you call culture. It accompanies you everywhere, in or out of the university, I have always seen you two together, arm in arm. I swear, I have seen you."

He straightened up his back and, with a semi-serious expression, added:

"I always trust the images that pop into my mind more than those I witness with my own eyes, and I can assure you I have seen you two together."

The professor managed to look at him with indulgence.

"But there is another image you have always evoked in me, by some odd association of ideas. Can you guess what it is?"

The professor tried:

"A ram?"

"No!" Salutati exclaimed. "How easy it is to lapse into self-delusion! No, my dear, you could be anything but a ram."

"No," Salutati continued. "I see an immense pyramid with a sparrow on its tip. I have read in some book that this sparrow comes to rest on its tip every thousand years, and at that time it gives it one single peck. At the very instant it has razed it to the ground, only one day of eternity will have gone by."

"The image in the book was a little different, but it

doesn't matter," the professor said. "Still, I would like to know what it has to do with me."

"To me, you are that sparrow, except that you never fly away. You are always there, steadfastly perched on the tip."

The professor nodded, in silence. Salutati touched his shoulder with his hand.

"I am just joking, my dear, you don't mind, do you?"

Then, slightly altering the tone of his voice, he added:

"On the other hand, it is absolutely true that I would like you a touch softer, more fragile. You know, I have noticed you have a tendency to use the same sort of adjectives over and over again."

A faint blush colored the professor's cheeks when he turned toward him.

"Is that so?"

"Please, please, don't get upset," Salutati answered, withdrawing his hand from the professor's shoulder and putting it next to his other one on his knees. "I am not saying anything extraordinary. You know I have a certain spirit of observation," he lowered his voice, as if he were going to reveal a secret, but of no consequence, "which, in the end, is nothing more than the ability to notice a particular thing and to ignore what surrounds it. Indeed, if I can see certain things it is because, in fact, I am absent-minded."

"Please go on."

"So, as I was saying," Salutati sighed. "You seem to favor what I would define as 'muscular' adjectives, such as 'strong,' 'robust,' 'vigorous,' 'potent,' and others of the same ilk."

"Of course," the professor exclaimed. "And I will

keep favoring them for as long as strength is considered a quality."

"Indeed, but you shouldn't get carried away," Salutati answered, placing a hand on his arm. "Strength is not always a quality. There are other important aspects in life. Besides, the other half of strength is often weakness. Look at me."

The professor looked at him. "I have survived illness because I have a weak constitution, used to fighting against almost everything. Otherwise I would have been crushed at the first blow."

"Certainly," the professor said.

Salutati looked baffled for a moment, but then went on:

"The other kind of adjectives you seem to relish refer to fencing weapons. Above all, 'incisive,' from the Latin 'incidere,' which shares the same root as 'occidere,' to kill, as my surgeon knows all too well. But it also means 'scratching,' 'cutting,' 'piercing.'"

"Agreed," the professor nodded. "But don't forget that even 'style' comes from stylus, an instrument used for writing when it was still incisive."

"Why don't you ever use adjectives such as 'loveable' or 'sweet'?" Salutati asked him as if he hadn't heard a word of what the professor had just said. "Have you ever used the adjective 'gentle'? Would you use it? Tell me."

"No," the professor patiently answered.

"See? On the other hand, am I wrong or are things changing?" Salutati asked him with a knowing look. "The surface of the lake is rippling, the first autumnal winds are blowing. Could it be a foreboding? What do you say?"

The professor listened to him with folded arms and a kindly expression on his face.

"The entire world is aging. *Mundus ipse senescit.* Everything is deteriorating and collapsing both within and without. Is that what you are feeling?"

"Of course, my dear, you may as well say it," Salutati went on, smiling.

He put his face close to the professor's:

"But that is wrong. We are the ones who are aging."

He lowered his voice and added:

"Admit it, you'll see how good it feels. When we have come this far, all that's left us is truth. A most detestable companion, I agree."

"I have never been afraid of it," the professor said.

"Of course not," Salutati said. "You don't know it. You have only just begun to open your eyes!"

The professor looked at him with a friendly smile:

"I'm no longer sure I know what you are talking about."

"Neither am I. And yet, we understand each other."

"Do you want me to tell you what I think of you?"

"Never!" Salutati exclaimed. "You and everybody else can think anything you want, just make sure you don't tell me."

The professor smiled:

"You're really trying to get to me tonight, aren't you?"

"True, but not just tonight. Tonight I am letting you know."

He squeezed the professor's shoulder.

"When I see you, surrounded by your students," he went on. "You, their professor and their friend, as we all know, always willing to lend them an ear. And then, suddenly, I realize that your eyes have stopped seeing them, that they have become glassy, maybe while you are nodding, listening to them, or maybe while you are once more pretending to correct them, with your usual: 'This is very true, to a great extent, but. . .' Tell me, what is really true, for you, at that moment? I think you see them all as dead."

"Dead?"

"Yes, dead. Both you and they, all dead. This is your sense of reality."

The professor sighed.

"What you are telling me now is quite interesting," he said. "I don't know whether it is true or not, but it could be."

"You see?" Salutati said. "The mere mention of death brightens up your eyes, makes them sparkle."

The professor nodded:

"Maybe."

"Believe me, you have improved," Salutati continued, resting his arm on the back of the sofa. "Some time ago you would have never admitted it. You are actually beginning to live. Do you know what animals do before an earthquake?"

"They become very restless, I suppose."

"They even come out of hibernation. They sense that the earth is about to cave in and they come out in the open."

"So what sort of animal do you think I am?"

"A badger," Salutati answered. "A well-fed, cautious badger."

"And what would cause the earthquake? Maybe the anonymous letter, is that it?"

Salutati, who was pulling himself up to find a more comfortable position on the sofa, froze midway as if he had just been stabbed in the back.

"You brought it up!" he exclaimed. "I hadn't even thought of it."

"Really?"

"Yes, really. On the other hand, my dear, since we have broached the subject why don't we talk about it?"

He made himself more comfortable in the corner of the sofa, resting one arm on the back and the other on a cushion.

"I read your answer in the magazine," he went on. "Do you want to hear what I think of it?"

"Sure."

Salutati concentrated for a moment, his eyes closed. When he reopened them, he said, very quickly, in a sigh:

"The tone was wrong."

While the professor, disappointed, bowed his head, Salutati went on:

"I found your attempt at being light-handed a little, how shall I put it, thick-ankled. How could you possibly say: 'It has aroused my curiosity'? Your curiosity?! Aroused by a cowardly letter?! Remember, only what is plausible can be convincing. That way you let others understand not only that you have been cut, but that you have been cut to the quick. By so doing, you have considerably weakened your position. Everybody agrees."

"Who is everybody?"

"Your colleagues, your friends," Salutati answered nonchalantly. "Still, you shouldn't let it bother you too much."

"Of course," he added. "It would have been better if you had ridiculed your attacker, but your answer..." and he raised his blue eyes on him.

"Falls short, is that what you were going to say?" the professor anticipated him.

"Well, let's just say that it reinforces his position," Salutati answered. "He will reply."

"You think so?"

"I am sure of it," Salutati answered, staring him in the eyes. "I am more than sure of it. Unless, of course, he dies. If he does not answer and one of your friends dies, you needn't look any further. Remember this."

"I will remember it," the professor said.

At that moment the doorbell rang and, shortly afterwards, uncertain as to whom he should greet first, the professor or Salutati, and, as a result, remaining where he was on the rug, Sivieri made his appearance in the hall.

"I'm glad I am not the first one," he said, vaguely bowing at both.

Tall, scrawny, with a crew-neck sweater and a monkish crown of hair around his bare skull, Sivieri was so perfect a caricature as to appear implausible. His greatest gift was his ability to exploit the most predictable aspects of his interlocutors: he flattered powerful men, complimented beautiful women, winked at ruffians, and, as for men of letters, he succeeded where even the best stand-up comedians failed, and that is, in caricaturing them, except that the caricature was himself. Thus, he had made a career for himself: he was a poet, a writer, and a critic, but, above all, he was innocent. He embodied what people, who usually did not associate with him, imagined as a *man of letters*, a seminarian with promise in his eyes. Banality drew him like an abyss, the ultimate deadline, a fatal rendezvous. He felt its presence with the excitement of a lecher confronting a perfect opportunity or the approach of pleasure. On such occasions, he would inevitably say "at the risk of sounding banal," or else, with firm bright eyes, "I know I am being banal," and he never failed.

His company was both sought and avoided for exactly the same reasons: he was the ideal person to fill someone else's absence, but his was never felt. No one knew for sure whether he was aware of this.

"I hope this won't last too long," Sivieri said.

"It won't if we stick to the point, my friend," Salutati answered. He had stood up, as had the professor, and had gone over to the fireplace.

"Have you already chosen a name?" Sivieri asked. "I beg your pardon, a motto. We should respect anonymity."

"Yes," Salutati answered.

"Who?"

"A poet who signs *In hoc signo vinces*."

"*Hoc signo vinces*," Sivieri delicately corrected him.

"No, *In hoc signo vinces*," Salutati insisted. "He has asked me for my support in the competition."

"Ah," Sivieri smiled maliciously.

"Indeed, but he has other qualities as well," Salutati said. "He may be a little too crepuscular, too somber, but he is so young. I'm sure he'll soon learn to smile."

He looked at the professor and at Sivieri, both still standing, and added:

"We are closer to childhood than they are. The less room life leaves us, the more we make for it inside. Do either of you ever think of your childhood, really?" he asked, turning toward the professor. "I do. Look."

He pulled a crocodile wallet from his jacket pocket, opened it up, and, from one of the slots, drew out a rectangular picture: a curly-haired, slightly bow-legged child was just letting go of the support from a round stone table and, with open arms, was lunging onto the gravel toward the photographer. His body, stretched forward, looked as if about to fall.

"And so I did fall, immediately afterwards," Salutati noted. "Still, look at the determination on my face, and at that rapacious hand as I am going for the camera. A small, fragile monster in movement. How I recognize myself in him, and how true it still is."

"What do you mean by 'true'?" Sivieri asked.

"Look at this other one," Salutati said.

He pulled another picture out of the same slot. It was smaller, square, and had a glossy finish with a white frame and serrated edges. The same child, arms wide open and mouth agape, was soaring at the level of a chandelier just before dropping back into the two hands, protruding from the lower margin of the photo, which had presumably bounced him up there.

"This was my father's favorite pastime," Salutati said with a glint in his eyes. "To see the terror in my eyes, and then save me. But I liked it too, I remember. Only a psychologist could doubt it."

He put both pictures back into the wallet, put it back in the inside pocket of his jacket, and pressed it with his hand.

"To me, these snapshots are absolutely extraordinary," he added. "Everything is so vivid, and so simple. They say that in the end our entire life flashes in front of our eyes like a movie. But, tell me, how can I even hope to make *In hoc signo vinces* understand this sort of thing? He has just started his movie. All I can do for him is give him my vote." He glanced at them over his glasses and added: "And yours. Why aren't we sitting down?"

As they were sitting down, he asked:

"Tell me, Sivieri, have you already found your favorite?"

Sivieri made a vague gesture with his hand and said:

"I haven't been particularly impressed by anyone."

"And what about you?"

211

The professor's eyes grew suddenly smaller:

"Yes, there is a girl who signs *Sit tibi terra levis.*"

"Oh!" Salutati exclaimed. "Our blessings for the dead. Did you suggest it to her?"

"No," the professor firmly answered. "In fact, I don't like it."

Raising his head with sudden energy, Salutati asked:

"And who is she?"

"We cannot mention any names," the professor answered. "In fact, we shouldn't even be aware of them. The title of the collection is *Gashes.*"

"Do you know her?"

"No."

"So how do you know it is a girl?"

"One can understand it from her poetry."

Salutati looked at him with the face of one torn between intense distress and utter disbelief:

"You're not going to tell me that you really like it?"

The expression on the professor's face was impenetrable.

"That vestal?" Salutati insisted, nonplussed.

"That unraped Sabine?" he added, raising the pitch of his voice.

"That harbinger of the apocalypse?" he went on, looking increasingly inspired, shifting his eyes from the professor's impassive face to Sivieri's inane smile.

"That astral lament?" he exclaimed. "You!" he turned toward the professor with a raised index finger and a threatening look. "You cannot be the accomplice to such an outrage to good taste. You know the creative power of words. So how can you propose we vote for *Gashes*?"

The professor rested his eyes on Sivieri's smile and said:

"All right, all right. But there is something to it."

"There is always something to everything," Salutati said.

"No, that's not what I meant."

Salutati edged closer to him and with a confidential tone, as if he were about to tell him a secret, whispered:

"It's worthless!"

Then he stared at him, as if waiting for his reaction, but as soon as the professor opened his mouth, he again repeated, in a whisper:

"Worthless!"

"Come on," the professor protested.

# XVIII

"But what did he say? Exactly," the girl asked. She had placed her handbag on the chair next to hers and was now watching the professor as she stirred her coffee with a little spoon.

"I have already told you," the professor answered, stroking the edge of the table with his hand. "You know Salutati. A stream of unrelated images. It is impossible to follow him."

She kept staring at him suspiciously.

"What sort of images?"

"Now I can't remember," the professor answered absent-mindedly, shaking his head. "Anyway, nothing offensive."

He pushed the table with his right hand and then, with his left foot, tried to smooth down a fold in the rug.

"He sort of hinted at a certain kind of poetess," he added.

"Are we still at that level?" the girl asked. "We are still distinguishing between poets and poetesses?"

"So it would seem."

"But you said that he expressed himself in images."

"True, I did," the professor answered, looking at the end of the balcony where a small wooden staircase led down to the bar on the ground floor.

"Please, don't behave as you usually do. Don't beat around the bush. I want to know the truth, you know I am not afraid of it."

"Now I remember," the professor answered. "He referred to a mournful note."

"Where?"

"In your poems."

"So, where is the image?"

The professor shrugged his shoulders.

"I don't know!" he exclaimed. "I told you I couldn't remember. Wrong, I remember one word," he added with a resigned look. "He said 'vestal.' "

The girl blushed and drew her face away, as if he had slapped her.

" 'Vestal'? Is that what he said?"

"Yes."

"And what did you say?"

"Me?" the professor asked. "How could I possibly answer such a man? I cannot meet him on his own ground, that quagmire of divagation. It would mean suicide. Nor can I lay my own cards on the table," he added, lowering his voice. "Anyway, I defended you."

"How?"

"No need to get into details. Anyway, the authority one puts in one's voice is always more eloquent than what one says." The girl remained silent, staring at the sugar bowl.

"Besides, discussions of literary texts!" the professor

216

added, completing his sentence with a hiss through his teeth.

After a pause, the girl asked him:

"Is he supporting someone?"

"Yes, someone who signs *In hoc signo vinces*."

The girl hesitated:

"Have you read his stuff?"

"Yes."

"How is it?"

The professor deliberated for a while and then answered:

"Not bad."

"You mean, good."

Pretending it cost him a big effort, the professor said:

"Yes."

The girl again hesitated, then, without looking at him, asked:

"Better or worse than mine?"

"You are asking me to draw an impossible comparison. You are still a little. . ." looking at her, he started raising the hand that was resting on the table, but did not proceed.

"A little what?"

The professor knitted his brow.

"A little immature," he answered. "You talk too much about yourself in other people's words. It will be much better when you talk to other people in your own words. But it takes time."

The girl stared blankly into space:

"Maybe you are not aware of how much you depress me when you talk to me this way. Every time I have to start anew."

"But that is what writing is all about."

"Yes, but you've got to start somewhere. Whereas

217

after I talk to you, I always feel I have to start from scratch."

In the meantime, the waiter had walked to their table and had placed the bill under the sugar bowl.

"Would you like to drink something else?"

The girl shook her head.

"I would like some mineral water," the professor said.

As the waiter walked away, the girl, with the same vacant stare, said:

"I'd rather not think about it."

"But what did I say that was so negative?"

"Nothing."

Then, she glumly added:

"Rather talk about concrete things."

"I'm listening."

"Does this mean that I won't even get an honorable mention?"

The professor shrugged his shoulders.

"Maybe you will."

"What does 'maybe' mean?" the girl asked. "Yes or no?"

"It means I hope you will."

"Why are you always so evasive?"

"That's what you think, because you are so insecure," the professor answered. "But I am not evasive."

"Then answer me: is it true or not that you were counting on the support of a few other members of the jury?"

"Yes, it is true."

"And they had promised you their votes."

"Yes and no."

"There you go again!"

"Not at all," the professor exclaimed. "It is not my fault if this is the way men are."

"You still believe that if it is not 'yes' it has got to be 'no,'" he continued. "But, in fact, most men are both 'yes' and 'no.'"

The girl shrugged her shoulders.

"I know that."

"No, you think you know it, but you have never really experienced it," the professor said. "You may even believe that it's quite an achievement to point out that men are 'yes' and 'no' at the same time. Easy, isn't it?"

The girl was looking at him, somewhat surprised:

"But isn't that what you just said?"

"No. They are 'yes,' and then again, maybe, they are 'no,' and then again 'yes' three times in a row, and then again 'no' and 'no.' They are never what you expect, and you never know what they will be. That's why I don't know whether they are going to vote yes or no."

He looked at her and added:

"You aren't convinced? Why do you always take it out on me?"

"Because you are always so ambiguous," the girl answered. "I never know what you are really thinking."

"Neither do I."

The girl smiled and gave a slight shrug of her shoulders. Then she looked at her watch.

"Are you going to work this evening?"

"No."

"In that case why don't we go have a cool drink on my terrace?" she proposed. "This way you'll finally see the studio I share with my friend. We won't be late."

"Splendid idea," the professor answered, getting up from his chair.

"But this is a real terrace!" the professor exclaimed, his nose in the air, taking in the warmth of the evening. He had just emerged from a small room and now found himself in the center of a large area of red tiles. He walked over to the parapet. Below him, the city was a vast brazier of sparkling lights.

"It's nice here, isn't it?" the girl said. "I'm going to get something to drink."

She went back into the house, stooping to pass through the low door.

"Here we are," she said after a while. "Want to come?"

She had placed a tray with a bottle of wine and a few bottles of soda on a table.

"Splendid," said the professor, letting himself drop on a deck chair.

"What would you like to drink?"

"A glass of white wine, please."

After pouring him the glass of wine the girl stood by, watching him:

"I wanted to talk to you for a second, just one more second, about that poem."

"All right," the professor said, resting his head against the back of the chair. "I'm listening."

"Wait, I don't have it here with me, let me get it," the girl answered, walking back toward the apartment.

A bat was flying through the television antennas clustered at the end of the terrace.

Back with her manuscript, the girl sat down on her deck chair and, resting her elbows on her knees, said:

"I am going to read you another version."

She cleared her throat, then, with a muted voice, she recited:

"The breakwater line, sea of weeds. . ."

"No, please," the professor interrupted her. "Don't start from the beginning, just read me the line."

"But you won't understand. Do you remember the rest?"

"Yes, I do."

The girl turned the page, sighed, and with the same doleful voice read:

"The unmotivated silence, explosion of
anguish"

The professor fixed his pensive eyes on the fake gas-lamp that hung right above the door.

"I don't like it," he said. "Anguish does not explode."

"Why not? Today the word 'explode' can mean a thousand different things. We even use it for the seasons: 'the explosion of summer.' "

"Still, I don't like it. To explode comes from *ex-plaudo* and implies a loud noise."

"Forget your etymologies," the girl exclaimed. "I'm using today's language."

"I know. And that is precisely what I don't like."

The girl stared at him:

"At times you are really detestable."

She plucked up her courage:

"Let me continue. I have eliminated the last stanza."

"Great. I did not like the image of the slides."

"So, why didn't you tell me earlier?"

"I thought I had hinted as much."

"No! You had only told me that the word 'slides'

did not convince you. But you had also said that it could well be a first reaction."

The professor shook his head.

"You should never trust what your readers say," he said. "Their reticence, the expressions on their faces are often far more eloquent than their words. And if they tell you that something does not convince them, what they really mean is that it nauseates them."

The girl bowed her head over the page:

"Anyway, I have eliminated that sentence."

"Fine, when you eliminate something it always works."

He looked at her and added.

"I was only joking. Please don't get mad."

"You like to tell me these things, don't you?"

"No, no, I told you I was only joking. Besides, if, as you say, you want to be treated as an equal, then I must be able to talk to you quite openly."

"Yes, but you don't have to wound me," the girl answered. "I want honesty, not brutality."

"I think you want too many things at the same time," the professor said, picking up his glass.

"That's not true. I just want an attitude based on solidarity and trust."

"Maybe I am too old for that," the professor said.

"Age has nothing to do with it. Daverio relates to young people in a completely different way."

"So, why don't you go consult with him?"

"You'd deserve it," the girl answered, staring at the parapet. "He is totally neurotic, but he is much more human than you."

She turned toward him and, after a pause, said:

"You know what you are like?"

"No," the professor answered, clutching the armrests with his hands.

"You are like a dead lake. I saw one last fall, there wasn't a single fish in it. I immediately thought of you."

"Many thanks," the professor said.

"One last thing," the girl said, emerging from the apartment with an ashtray in her hand. One could hear the whirring of crickets in the distance. "And then, I promise, I won't say anything else. I've got an idea for a science-fiction story. Want to hear it?"

"Sure," the professor said.

"One day, a man discovers by chance that he has the power to kill people from a distance, merely by thinking of them. So, first he bumps off his wife, then two of his friends, then his mother."

The professor was listening to her attentively.

"Then he starts choosing his victims haphazardly," the girl went on. "He goes out at night and snuffs out all the people he meets."

"How does it end?"

"After a while he kills all the men and is the only male left in the city. Then he starts killing the women. Do you find it interesting?"

"Yes, but I want to know how it ends."

"In the end he is left alone in the world. Until the day when, thinking casually about himself, he causes his own death."

"Excellent," the professor said.

# XIX

Feeling inside his jacket pocket with his right hand while standing in the bus with his belly pressed against the window, the professor found the corner of the envelope and, pulling it out with difficulty, opened it. Bending his body forward to protect it from accidental shoves and pushes, he placed the letter against the window and, reading it, learned that his wife was cheating on him.

A sudden stop of the bus sent him crashing against the window, and he found himself with his nose only a couple of inches away from the letter. Enlarged by his glasses, the words he reread at the level of his mouth were "surprises" and "Benedetto Marcello." Once the bus had again started up, he managed to slide the letter down the pane and hide it in the pocket of his trousers. He felt as if he were going to faint. Instead of speeding up, his heartbeat was slowing down and the boulevard was becoming a luminous strip spangled with dots. He closed his eyes. A hand grabbed his arm and a voice asked him:

"What's the matter? Are you all right?"

"Yes, yes," he stammered. "I am going to be fine."

"Would you like to sit down?" the old man sitting across from him asked.

"No, thank you," he answered with a steadier voice. "I am getting out here."

He got out among the blurred, unrecognizable highrises of Piazza Tricolore, and immediately entered the dark hallway of a bar.

"What would you like to have, sir?" somebody asked him from the counter.

"An espresso," he managed to say as he sat at a table.

By and by, things reacquired contour, luminous dots and colored splotches disappeared, and he saw a yellow cab drive slowly along the sidewalk. Then, as his breathing quieted down, he realized that the danger was over and that another bad spell had just started.

As soon as he found himself in his office on campus, the professor locked both door and window, let himself drop into a chair, and pulled the letter out of his pocket.

Do you like surprises?
If so, follow your wife
to Via Benedetto Marcello 27.
We are always betrayed.

The professor clutched his head with his hands.

"Calm down," he said.

He saw her by the window, turning to face him:

226

"How could you believe it?"

"But I didn't."

Seated in the armchair, she was saying:

"How could you believe an anonymous letter!"

He rubbed the fingers of his right hand across his face and drew them back, damp.

"You are crazy," she said, wriggling in her seat.

He stood up, went to the window, and opened it. A pigeon immediately took off from the sill and flew to the dome. The word "surprises" was also in the other letter. With a gasp, the professor stopped in the middle of the room and leaned against the desk. That's who it was. It was the other.

Shivering all over, the professor slumped into his chair. And yet, he felt his suspicions were wrong. It could not be the same person. The other was an enemy, this one was a wretch. The other kept his distance, this one annihilated it with the sordid familiarity of anonymous letters, intended to bring the addressee down to the level of the writer, the better to strike at him. No, he should not confuse the two senders. Some people experienced a visionary pleasure in sending anonymous letters. He remembered one of his neighbors, an old, monumental woman, who had been rescued from the streets when still young by a water commissioner who had inexplicably decided to marry her. The loss of a precise vocation, the impossibility of offering her own huge body to whoever craved it, had been the secret regret of her entire life. In her dotage, she had started sending anonymous letters concerning imaginary adulteries to all her neighbors. Caught and tried, she had been sentenced to a light penalty by an understanding judge. She was the sort of person who could have written the last sentence, "We are always betrayed," since she was apt to say, whether as an alibi, an assessment, or both at once: "love always betrays us."

The certainty that the two letters had not been written by the same person lifted a large weight off his chest. He sighed and put his glasses back on. But, suddenly, a different fear cut the breath in his throat: what if the letter had spoken the truth?

At that very moment, somebody rapped on his door. "Who is it?"

"It's me," the assistant softly answered.

Spreading his arms in resignation and raising his eyes to the ceiling, the professor put the letter back in his pocket and went to open the door.

"What's the problem?" he asked him.

"I'm here to go over those exams, Professor," the assistant answered, walking to the center of the room.

"Not today, please. I don't feel like it."

"What's the matter, Professor?" asked the assistant, who had sat down on a chair, a briefcase on his knees.

"I am not feeling very well."

"This has been going on for a some time, hasn't it? Maybe it is some form of exhaustion."

"Maybe," the professor answered, raising his eyes to him. "Why? You have noticed it?'

"Yes, and I am not the only one."

"Who else has?" the professor asked impatiently. "Tell me their names, I am sick and tired of anonymity!"

The assistant turned pale.

"I don't like to reveal names," he said. "In any case, more than one person."

"And you, what do you think?"

"What do you want me to tell you?"

"What you think, of course," the professor answered, as the veins in his neck started swelling. "But, first of all, try to think!"

Mustering as much dignity as he could, the assistant closed his briefcase and got up.

"You might have your reasons to be so upset, Professor," he said calmly. "But you should also realize that you are offending me."

"Offending you! You must be joking!" the professor answered somewhat surprised. He gestured toward a chair with his arm and added:

"Please sit down, what are you doing?"

"I understand you are going through very difficult times," the assistant continued, standing. "But this morning you are overdoing it."

"Maybe you are doing the same thing," the professor suggested. "In any case, I apologize."

"Don't you want to sit down?" he added.

The assistant moved his chair back a few inches and then sat down.

"I didn't know you were so sensitive," the professor went on. "I am sorry."

The assistant nodded:

"All right."

"But you must admit that you are a little too evasive," the professor said. "You are too diplomatic for your own good."

The assistant raised his eyes.

"Who do you think you are, Cardinal Mazzarin?" the professor asked.

The assistant tightened his lips:

"There you go again!"

"No, not at all," the professor answered. "But don't think others don't see through you. Psychology doesn't work."

"What do you mean?"

"I am alluding to psychology used as a tactical tool," the professor answered. "Other people know exactly how you are. Particularly those who work with you. If they appreciate you, it is because you are fine the way you are, and not because of any act you put on."

The professor rested his head against the wall.

"In other words, all your performances are useless," he added. "As is your evasiveness, or whatever else. Anyway, at this particular moment, do you know how I feel about other people's opinion?"

"Indifferent."

"Right. It leaves me totally indifferent."

"Do you hear me?" he added. "In-dif-fer-ent."

He removed his glasses and massaged his closed eyelids with the fingers of his right hand.

"So, you want to postpone the correction of the exams?"

"Right!" the professor energetically exclaimed, popping his eyes wide open. "I've more important things to take care of in the next couple of days. For my own sake. Do you follow me?"

As he walked along Via Benedetto Marcello, between two rows of uneven houses and low villas surrounded by gardens, the professor was inexplicably, if absolutely, sure that number 27 was the cylindrical highrise that, shrouded in haze, towered at the end of the street. He stopped in front of a service station. A cool draft of air issued from the underground garage. He wiped the sweat off his brow with the back of his hand and, raising his face, closed his eyes. Why had she told him where she was going as she left? Generally she didn't say anything. He kept walking along the sidewalk. The hot air rising from the street rippled the outline of the highrises. Sweat kept trickling down his body. Clarity is the basis of all relationships. You agree with that, don't you? They were sitting in an outdoor restaurant on the lake shore. You mean, no secrets, no lies, he had asked her. Yes, she had answered. The scampering on the gravel at his right told him that a dog was rushing against a gate. He did not turn around to look at it as it went on barking behind him. But you are so diffident! Will you be able to be sincere? she had asked him. Two stone cats curled on top of the gateposts. He had reached villa number 95, a real fortress. The sidewalk was blocked off. He stepped down the curb and walked on in the street. I haven't yet understood whether you believe in fidelity, she had told him. It was midnight, they had just come out of the Eden theater and were waiting to cross the street. Do you? he had asked her. Yes, I do.

He stopped on the curb and wiped his glasses. Whereas you believe in betrayal, she had suddenly added, looking at him. No, why? he had answered, surprised but also relieved at her having intuited the truth. He heard a car approaching from behind and immediately climbed back onto the sidewalk. Number 75 was a cubical house. Next came an abandoned building with all the panes broken out of the windows, and a rundown façade on which a few faded letters still spelled out *Armenian-Mekhitarist House.*

The car pulled over next to him and a man stuck his head out the window.

"Would you happen to know where Via Lepanto is?"

"No, I don't," he answered.

His lips felt parched, just like his throat. Maybe

number 27 was not the highrise: he had already reached number 55 and the highrise was still quite far off.

He walked by the fence. Always expect the worst. Sivieri, his eyes beaming stupidity, had said: "There is always salvation, a door opening." He passed his handkerchief over his face. What salvation? What door?

A black strip of tar, hot and glistening, rippled the air in front of him. All this because of a letter that was probably lying. You are used to duplicity, but I am not. They were walking downstairs. Duplicity? Yes, whereas I could never cheat on you. At worst, I'd leave you.

Number 27 was a one-story house, with a sloping roof and a window with half-opened shutters. An unexpected puff of wind caused the white curtains to billow into the darkness inside. He walked slowly to the gate and, absent-mindedly, tried to push it open, but it was locked. He walked on. An old woman was watching him from the opposite sidewalk. He stared at her and she hesitatingly moved on. But when he turned around, she was still looking in his direction. He pulled his wallet from his jacket pocket and pretended to be looking for something. Raising his eyes, he saw the old woman walk away.

He put the wallet back in his pocket and slowly walked on. At the end of the fence he noticed a passage between the last pickets and the wall surrounding the next house. He sneaked in and proceeded across the grass and gravel. A small rusty gate, half-hidden under a rotting wood roof, blocked a path leading to the side of the villa. Inside, he saw a wheelbarrow tilted over a mound of sand. Maybe they were going to build a wall. He leaned against the bars with his hands and the gate swung open. Then he almost ran across the gravel to the small concrete sidewalk that surrounded the house. He stopped under the eaves, pressed against the wall, panting.

He stood there for a while, sweat dripping down his face, catching his breath. A tall wall, entirely covered with ivy, rose immediately behind the house and hid him from sight.

As soon as he had recovered, he started creeping along the wall, past the closed shutters of the first window, all the way to the second one. The shutters of this one were only half-closed. He heard some noise inside. He craned his neck, the palms of his hands clinging to the stucco, his knees jammed against a little bench that stuck out of the wall. A young man was speaking with a voice so low as to be almost inaudible.

"Are you sure?" the young man asked, suddenly raising his voice. But the answer that reached him through the window was only a vague murmur, as of a voice being hushed, then:

". . . ing."

". . . stand."

He could not figure out whether the woman's voice was really hers. The young man had started talking again, softly. Then, suddenly, and quite clearly, he said:

"But it is absurd."

Her answer went on for quite a while, but even pricking up his ears he couldn't make out a single word, just confused sounds, broken by frequent pauses: yes, generally her talk was interspersed with pauses. Total silence ensued, then the rustle of a body slipping out of bed, bare footsteps on the floor. A door knob was turned and the steps receded. When they came back he heard the noise of a body climbing back into bed. Then a diffused rubbing, an isolated moan, and sultrier, heavier breathing:

"Darling."

He climbed onto the bench, no longer afraid of being discovered, and, stretching toward the opening between the two shutters, finally managed to see.

Whenever, much later, he thought back on that moment, he would always feel a vague tremor and see the same image: her naked body, so white in the darkness, slowly lifting, slowly moving. Only later did he realize that he had already seen that same scene several years earlier, in a science-fiction movie, in which a monstrous being, sallow and pasty, writhed on a bed under the fearful, glittering eyes of a man. Eventually the man let himself sink into that whitish glob causing it to open up and entangle him in a long and flaccid struggle that quite sapped his energies. The body of the man finally managed to crush the shapeless, viscous being which immediately started spreading out under him.

He would have never recognized her from the raucous, intermittent sounds that issued from her lips, nor from the seemingly gigantic body he saw from where he stood. Only the face, on the pillow, surrounded by darkness was undeniably hers, even though somewhat transformed. He remembered his reactions as different from the ones he had expected. He had felt surprise rather than anger. The certainty that had suddenly put an end to his doubts had summarized itself in two words: "Of course." There was no turning back. Then gradually he had been seized by a strange thrill, a sort of suspense that had made him lean against the shutters with the palms of his

234

hands and had lent his eyes the feverishly furtive look of guilt. As for hatred, he had imagined it more than felt it. He had attributed to it the lump in the throat, the throbbing in his temples and the sudden onrush of blood that had veiled his eyes. But when, after a scream, she had stopped moving and her breath had become inaudible, he had felt relieved, as if freed and at peace. A warm light filtered through the leaves of the garden. He heard the flutter of wings soaring off the wall.

He climbed down from the bench very slowly so as not to make any noise. He tiptoed to the corner of the house and then walked to the gate. Here he spread out his handkerchief and, closing his eyes, applied it to his face. He kept it there until it grew wet. Then he rubbed it down his cheeks and reopened his eyes.

# XX

After waving at each other from afar, beyond the frantic flapping of pigeons relentlessly taking flight above the paving stones of the square, the professor and Salutati met under the dome of the War Memorial.

"So glad to see you," the professor said, as his mouth suddenly went dry. "How are you?"

"Fine and you?"

"Awful," the professor answered with a weak smile. "Difficult times."

"Why?"

"I don't know if I can trust you," the professor answered faltering.

"Absolutely not!" Salutati exclaimed.

Then he added:

"Let me explain, my dear," he rested his hand on the professor's shoulder. "If it is a secret you want to tell me," he paused, "don't. I have known myself too long, I thrive on other people's secrets, I am a voyeur of existence. On the other hand, if you need advice, I'll be glad to give it to you."

The professor hesitated:

"Why, whom could you possibly tell?"

"I might not tell anybody. But then again, I might. Or, if you really insist, I might cover up your tracks and cite your case as an *exemplum*, a circumstantial mishap."

Then, raising his voice, he added:

"Is it very serious?"

"Yes."

"Very private, personal?"

"Yes."

"Something, to cite a banal example, a merely hypothetical case, something akin to a wife's betrayal?"

The look in the professor's eyes wavered between diffidence and relief:

"Yes, something of that order."

He blinked a couple of times and then added:

"In fact, that's precisely it."

"Very well," Salutati said, glancing at his watch. "In that case I have half an hour. What would you say if we went to Ranzati. It's close by and fairly quiet."

A few minutes later, they were walking down the steps that led to a cool cellar lined with casks. They sat down in the back, at a worm-eaten wood table. As the waiter approached, Salutati said:

"Their wine is excellent, but this isn't the right time. I am going to have coffee. What about you?"

"Me too."

"Two coffees, one weak."

As the waiter walked away, shouting in the direction of the counter: "Two coffees, one weak," Salutati bent toward the professor, sitting still on his bench, and asked him:

238

"When did you find out?"

"This afternoon."

"Who is he?"

"Someone you know."

"Who? Daverio?"

"No, Daverio has nothing to do with it."

"Obviously not, if you say so."

"No, it is an ex-student of mine," the professor said, resting his forehead in the palm of his hand. "I am not one hundred percent sure, but the evidence points to him."

"Has he graduated?"

"Yes, he got a cum laude, from me," the professor answered. "He was one of my best students. Now and then he would even pay me a visit at home."

"See, one should never favor the best," Salutati said, staring at the approaching waiter. "The weak coffee is for me, the other goes to the professor."

He pulled a little bottle of saccharine pills out of his pocket and dropped one into his coffee. He took a sip and then asked:

"What's your real problem?"

The question yanked the professor out of the trance-like state in which he had been staring at his cup, and made him raise his head:

"Yes, yes, but first of all I would like to know what you think of it?"

"Think of what?"

"Of betrayal."

"Quite normal," Salutati answered after a minute's thought.

The professor looked at him with vague gratitude:

"Normal in what sense?"

"In the most literal sense, that is, it is part of the norm," Salutati answered, drinking his coffee and placing the cup back on its saucer. "The opposite is the exception, the outcome of an admirable series of casual circumstances."

"That's not what I gather," said the professor, perplexed. "At least not statistically."

"Do you believe statistics, or what you told me once, namely, that betrayal is at the basis of life?"

"I said that?"

"Yes. I remember you were very tired, utterly exhausted, and those are always the most lucid moments."

"I feel as if I were living in a different world," the professor answered, resting his chin on the back of his right hand. "I have the feeling I have been living with a monster."

"I understand," Salutati sighed. "That's exactly how she would have felt had she seen you with you know whom."

"With whom?"

"Please, please. Don't play games with me! At least not now," Salutati exclaimed, spreading out his arms.

The professor looked at him.

"You know something?"

"Yes!"

"What do you know?"

"Enough."

The professor was about to add something but Salutati went on:

"I don't see why you should be so surprised by your wife's behavior," he said. "Even though I can understand that discovering that she is just like you would be enough to pull the rug from under your feet."

"But then, why would she tell me that she was in love with me?"

Salutati looked at him perplexed.

"With you?"

"Yes. That's what she kept telling me."

Salutati concentrated for a while:

"You see, my dear, everything is possible in the realm of feelings, it's even possible that a woman as young and attractive as your wife should fall in love with a rodent like you, someone who only feeds on paper, constantly devouring print to turn it into more print."

"What are you trying to say? What's print got to do with it?"

"Please, don't interrupt me," Salutati said, putting his hand on his arm. "I know I'm painting a rather partial picture, but I think I have already explained to you the importance of changing one's point of view, at least now and then."

The professor listened to him in silence.

"Is it so surprising that a woman like her, beautiful and desirable, should, after five years of marriage, develop an interest in someone else?"

"No."

"Excellent. Nor is it so strange that she might even feel desire."

"No."

"Excellent," Salutati repeated, with satisfaction. "So, the question is not whether you fill her entire mental space. Such a thing never happens, even though all lovers hope so. The question, or rather, one of the questions, is whether the other fills more space than you do."

The professor was taken aback.

"I wouldn't know."

"You should look into this," Salutati continued. "On the other hand, if she is really in love with you, as she says she is, I don't think she will leave you."

241

"Leave me?!" the professor exclaimed, astounded. "If anything, I will leave her."

"Dear boy," Salutati indulgently replied, "when it comes to our relationships with others, we must always be ready for the worst. I tend to think that her interest in you could well coexist with her interest in someone else, that is, unless it has faded too much."

He drank his glass of water, and then asked:

"Did you suspect anything?"

"No," the professor shook his head. "Though now and then she would complain that I did not love her enough."

"True," Salutati noted. "Though, of course, it was also a way of attributing to you what she herself felt. She had everything she needed, the three crucial ingredients: the cause, the effect, and the future alibi."

The professor listened to him glumly.

"Now and then she would jokingly speak of temptations," he said. "But I never believed her."

"That is terrible!" Salutati exclaimed while summoning the waiter. "You must always believe what others say about themselves, at least on two occasions. First," and he stuck out the thumb of his right hand, "when they say that they are mediocre. Indeed, they are, my dear, they inevitably are. And second," and he raised the index finger of the same hand, "when they speak of temptations."

"Physical temptations, ephemeral matters. . ." the professor hesitated.

"What are you saying!?" Salutati exclaimed, and then, turning to the waiter and lowering his voice, added: "The check, please." "You mean to tell me that you still believe in language? Language can serve many purposes; it can be a means of defense, aggression, deception, and self-deception, but when it comes to understanding it is useless. Every word must be interpreted as if it were part of some archaic language. It's a relentless task. Besides, what do you mean by physical?"

"You don't believe in physical temptations?"

"Of course I do," Salutati said, studying the check. "I'm well aware of what they mean. Though, on second thought, maybe not that much. Anyway, just the word 'temptation' should have been sufficient to put you on your guard."

"What could I have done about it?"

"Not much, rest assured," Salutati answered. "The one who is about to betray always receives the definitive push from the betrayed. It is always the same story. A form of help that is as unconscious as it is inevitable."

The professor showed his agreement by nodding his head.

"Besides, relationships. . . ," Salutati said but did not finish the sentence. "The mind is brittle, it deteriorates, it ages, it rots."

"And now, what do you think I should do?"

"Accept the situation," Salutati calmly replied. "Make as if nothing had happened. Only a lie can be perfect."

He pulled out his wallet, re-examined the check, and then slipped a few bills under the saucer.

"You may have a tendency to accept too much," the professor said.

"True," Salutati solemnly agreed. "I have spent the first fifty years of my life rejecting everything, and now I am spending whatever time I've left accepting everything. Mentally, of course."

"You are not a reliable source," the professor said with regret. "Not only do you accept things as they are, but you don't even try to interpret them. All you care about are facts."

"Yes, I adore literary facts. A hundred explanations and none of them effective."

He looked at his watch and added:

"I must run along now."

As they walked toward the exit, the professor concluded:

"So, you think I should be accepting."

"Yes. I know it is hard, but that is all you can do. You'll see, things will go on as before."

"I shouldn't say anything."

"Nothing."

The professor had stopped in the alley:

"You try to do the same, please. Don't tell anybody what I have told you. Please."

Salutati smiled.

"Old boy, you shouldn't ask what's impossible. But I promise, that if I mention it, nobody will be able to recognize you."

When he got home, it was already dark. She met him at the door.

"Why are you so late? Did something happen?"

"No. I am just terribly tired."

He placed his hat on the coatrack, next to his briefcase, and added:

"I would like to eat right away."

She hesitated at the living room door:

"Could we, maybe, talk for a minute?"

"Now?" the professor asked.

"Yes."

"Is it important?"

"Yes."

The professor raised his arms.

244

"All right, then. What is it?"

"I know this is not exactly the right time," she said. "Nor the right way. . . ."

"So?"

"I would like a separation," she said.

Then she added:

"I would like a divorce."

"Do you remember the friend I told you about?" Daverio asked his wife, as she sat between him and the window in the half-empty car of a subway train.

"Which one?" she asked, looking out the window. "You have so many."

"The one who had an affair with the wife of one of his friends."

"You call that an affair?! Besides, I thought it was an imaginary case."

"Call it what you will, it doesn't matter," Daverio said as the train pulled into a station.

"You remember that he wanted to tell her about her husband's affair with another woman," he continued, "hoping it would rid him of his last rival?"

"Yes, I remember."

"Well, things have taken an unexpected turn," Daverio said with a faint smile.

In the meantime, the doors had opened to let the last passengers in.

"Yes, something has happened that he would have never expected," he added. "And it has thrown him for a loop."

"In other words, she has somebody else."

"Exactly. How did you guess?"

"Oh, it was awfully hard."

The train had started moving again and the lights

along the tunnel turned into an uninterrupted, incandescent beam.

"She has asked her husband for a divorce," Daverio said.

She cuddled up against the window.

"And your friend, what is he going to do?"

Daverio bowed his head.

"I don't know," he answered. "I only know that he is in a terrible state."

"Can't he develop any other interests, at his age?"

"No, he can't develop any other interests. Obviously he can't."

"But then, he is sick."

"Quite possibly," Daverio answered. "Everybody is, one way or another."

The train had suddenly slowed down in mid-tunnel.

"Your friend is that weak?" she asked.

"Yes," Daverio answered. "And he is fully aware of it."

"He admits it?"

"Of course. It allows him to feel even weaker."

Her eyes briefly met his in the windowpane:

"But you think he is right."

"Yes, I do," Daverio answered, as if with resignation.

"All that just for a woman?"

"Yes."

She had pulled herself out of her corner:

"I no longer recognize you."

Daverio spread his hands out:

"What can I do?"

The train was now coming to a stop along a platform.

246

"You really think it is worth your while?" she asked him.

"No."

"But then?"

"Nothing else is."

"This is absurd."

"I don't think so," Daverio said. "Why are you so upset?"

"I am very calm," she exclaimed. "But you have lost your mind."

A group of children poured noisily into the car through the front door.

"It is like suicide," Daverio said. "One should never commit it because of someone else, and yet one does."

"Don't tell me you are defending it?"

"Of course," Daverio said. "It is a choice. At times I have trouble defending life."

"You're really no longer yourself, you know," she said, staring at him. "Why don't you try to react?"

"I am tired."

"Don't you think I'm tired too?"

Daverio leaned his head against the back of his seat.

"Tired of what?" he asked her.

"Of you, for instance."

Daverio nodded:

"You are right."

She turned again toward the window.

"And you? What are you tired of?"

"Of everything."

"Like your friend."

"Yes."

"So you can keep each other company."

Without raising his head from the back of the seat, Daverio turned to look at her.

"Except that he would be better off with someone else," he said.

"That is?"

"Someone a bit more vital, someone who could at least believe in what he is doing."

"Why, you don't believe in what you do?"

"No."

The train kept screeching throughout a curve.

"You don't even believe in your work?"

"No. I am even tired of writing."

"That's odd," she said.

"Why? It isn't any odder than liking it. It is just a question of energy."

"Your attitude used to be quite different."

"Of course. When you are young you are always busy, always full of motives. Death is far off."

As their stop approached, she stood up.

"And then?" she asked.

"Then, by and by, justifications are harder and harder to find," Daverio answered. "I first realized it as I started growing old."

"You have been obsessing about old age."

"Yes. I find it horrible. A terrible surprise."

She turned toward him as they stood in front of the door:

"You have just discovered that?"

"Not long ago," Daverio answered.

"And it isn't the only surprise," he added.

# XXI

Daverio killed himself one morning at daybreak, an hour the doctor said was quite typical. He had probably slept until five or so, as could be inferred by the barely rumpled state of the bed. A dream must have woken him up. The doctor, who lived on the floor below and had immediately answered the concierge's call, spoke with a very soft voice as he addressed the very upset woman who had accompanied him upstairs. Dreams, he had explained, are often responsible for precipitating the fatal deed at the very moment the victim is still trying to avoid it. Besides, there was no absolute certainty that this was a real suicide since Daverio was probably so accustomed to taking tranquillizers that he might have simply, and quite unconsciously, overdosed; on the other hand, the two empty bottles on the night-table rendered that hypothesis somewhat shaky.

Given the dose, death must have occurred in a matter of minutes. No, he had not suffered. Lying, as he was, on the sheets, wearing light pajamas, and with his arms resting comfortably by his sides, he looked as if he were asleep, at least according to the description of the concierge who had found him in the early afternoon when he had gone to clean the apartment. But, in fact, that was never the case, as the doctor noted the moment the concierge had gone to phone the police. People said it out of habit finding it easier to repeat what they had heard than to look with their own eyes. But a dead man was not asleep nor were the traits of any sleeper quite as motionless, imperturbable, absent. Daverio's head was propped up by a pillow and his parted lips could have given the impression, to someone walking through the hallway and casually glancing in, that he was trying to speak. But it would have been enough to walk into the bedroom to realize that he would never say another word. A few hours had already elapsed from the moment of his death, so it was useless to try to help him.

The room was in semi-darkness. Through the shutters, left ajar, filtered the gray light of a cloudy sky. Now and then, the curtains billowed in the cool breeze. He had probably left the window half-open when he had gone to sleep, a widespread but not very hygienic habit. Around dawn, as the temperature suddenly cools down, so does the body. Without that thermal variation, he might not have woken up. It was probable, the doctor suggested, that the suicide had not been premeditated. And, indeed, it lacked the most characteristic ingredient: a note for those who were left behind. This aspect was in itself enough seriously to question the hypothesis of deliberate intention. On the other hand, the victim was a man who, given his profession, was so used to writing that he might have well deluded himself into believing that he had already said, in so many ways and on different occasions, what he meant to say.

A travel book lay open on the night stand: *With the Togos in the Heart of Africa*. The upper portion of a green card, functioning as a book mark, was covered with a few names, listed in a column: Brydone, Wallenberg, Digby. These were followed by another illegible name, two dates—1770 and 1627—and a verb "to check." Such an impulse for scholarly precision seemed to exclude the anticipation of an imminent death. On the other hand, according to the doctor, this sort of behavior did not mean much. In fact, there are people who, even as they are dying, go on not believing in death, but in survival. Almost all suicides act as if they were not actually going to disappear. They set up appointments, deadlines, all those little things which, later, will keep recurring in the talk of relatives unwilling to accept the possibility of premeditation. And, indeed, the will could have wavered, leaving death a great deal of elbow room, or, more simply bracketing it, as it often does with life. This could have been the case with Daverio who had written "to check" just in case he still might go on living. Unless it was his way of confusing his and other people's ideas, and of protecting those he would leave behind against remorse. Nor was irony to be altogether excluded. The doctor knew Daverio superficially, having occasionally met him on the staircase or at condominium meetings. He saw him as an anxious man, a cyclothymic. What does cyclothymic mean, the

251

woman had asked. Someone who keeps oscillating between spells of euphoria and periods of depression, the doctor had answered. Ah, the woman pensively had replied, fully satisfied. It wouldn't have been the first time that a suicide, alienated from the rest of the world given his feeling of impending death, had, in his last moments, found the courage to make an inconsiderate joke. After all, it is the last liberty he can allow himself, and, in some cases, the first. And so his carefully laid-out corpse becomes an enigmatic, allusive presence troubling the house where it had, until then, lived above suspicion. The very possibility of anticipating or deferring death gives him a strange superiority, an unexpected freedom of movement. Those who give in to death cannot elude it, but those who choose it elude life, and this is one of the enduring charms of suicide.

It is very uncommon for a successful suicide not to be preceded by a failed one, the doctor maintained, and exceptional are the ones in which a failed suicide is not eventually followed by a successful one. The relatives of the victims generally fail to grant those earlier attempts the importance that they will eventually acquire in their memory after the success of the last one. But even in those instances they tend to speak of inevitability, momentary confusion, loss of consciousness. The main problem is to find the right word, and to repeat it until its meaning is forgotten. *Raptus* is one of the most common because it implies suddenness, suggests madness, and ignores pain. In its Latin form, *raptus* evokes an incomprehensible violence coming from the outside and overwhelming its victim after a short and vain resistance. And indeed, the doctor continued, would-be suicides who are caught in the act often look as if they are the objects of violence, not its perpetrators—hence, the common belief that they are, as it were, beside themselves, literally somebody else. He was no longer himself, the relatives insist. And in fact, the presence of someone else is often enough to break the spell, interrupt the metamorphosis, and invert it. Maybe even Daverio, had he been caught in the act by his wife, would have been unable to give any reason for his action. Indeed, had she been at home, he might not even have tried it.

There was a note in the bedroom, but it was his wife's. It was leaned up against the mirror, on top of the dresser. It said:

> Remember to turn off <u>both</u> gas taps before
> you go to sleep.

The word both had been underlined three times, a sign, according to the doctor, of both her apprehensiveness and his absent-mindedness. She must have been a very protective woman with a great need for affection, as indicated by the other notes left in the most strategic places throughout the apartment, and containing the address of the dry-cleaner, of the plumber, and, in the instance of the one pinned in the hallway, a reminder to bolt the door after locking it. Obviously she was afraid of all the dangers that could intrude from the outside world, but had probably failed to see the ones crouching within, in her own husband, left alone at home. Solitude can be fatal to those drawn to suicide. They think of themselves, of the day they may no longer be able to fend off death

but will no longer have to defend themselves against
life either, and all they have to do is surrender. In the
crease of Daverio's livid lips lurked a frozen, barely
perceptible smile, maybe a hint of his wish to give in
to temptation, at last.

# XXII

At the top of the wooden staircase that led to the balcony of the bookstore, the professor relieved himself of both his raincoat and his briefcase and wiped a few raindrops off his glasses. After testing them against the skylight, through which a dull gray light poured onto the clients on the first floor, he put them back on his nose and walked toward the section entitled *Chess,* where he knelt on the floor. He gently drew the second book out of the bottom shelf, carefully examined its front and back covers, and then opened it: it was *The Fundamentals of Chess* by Capablanca. He leafed through it slowly, occasionally readjusting his glasses and lingering on the figures, and then put it back on the shelf.

He then grasped the spine of the next book with his fingertips and carefully drew it out. The chessboard on its cover had been photographed from an unusual angle so as to appear as if it were expanding infinitely. Its title was *How Not to Play Chess,* and its text was a detailed analysis of the errors committed by the masters in the course of their most decisive games. With glittering eyes, the professor stood up and placed this book on top of those lined up along the top shelf.

Back on his knees, he put his face closer to the books in the bottom shelf and, running his index finger along their spines, he proceeded toward the end of the row until he found the title *Sacrifice in the Game of Chess*. He pulled the book out and quickly leafed through some of its chapters: "The function of sacrifice". . . "Sacrifice as ploy". . . "Sacrifice and profit". . . "Preventive sacrifice". . . "Sacrifice as simplification". . . "Unfortunate sacrifice." He placed this book on top of the other one and knelt back down. A book published by Dover commemorated the greatest games of the past. It was full of old pictures, mostly dark and out of focus, such as the one taken during the St. Petersburg Tournament of 1914: it showed Tarrasch and Lasker sitting in front of a chessboard and, standing behind them in different postures, Alekhin, Capablanca, and Marshall. Tarrasch, obviously about to make his move, was staring at the pieces while Lasker, his elbow on the table, his eyes gazing into the distance, looked very calm and confident. He started reading the account of a New York Tournament at the end of the nineteenth century:

> The snow that has been falling on our city for three solid days has transformed the mansion where the tournament is being held and its immense park into a silent white universe. This evening, in the sparkling Naiads Hall, on the second floor, the Romantic school and the Mod-

ern school will confront each other in their most superlative incarnations.

He put this book next to the other two. The rain had almost stopped falling and the rivulets snaking across the skylight had started thinning out.

"What are you doing, perched up there?"

He turned around and saw Salutati looking up at him from among the bookracks downstairs.

"I will be right down," he answered.

He slipped the briefcase under his arm, placed his raincoat on the other, took the three books in his hands, and, careful not to trip down the steep steps, descended to the first floor.

"Just look at you, as loaded down as a mule. Let me help you carry something," Salutati said taking the books from his hands. The professor went to put the briefcase on a shelf, next to the front door.

When he got back, Salutati was leafing through his books:

"I see you are still fascinated by chess."

"Yes."

"Do you play often? Are you good at it?" he asked, curious.

"No," the professor serenely answered. "I prefer retracing other people's games to playing."

"It doesn't surprise me," Salutati said. He had taken *Sacrifice in the Game of Chess* and was perusing it.

"Please excuse my ignorance," he said, "but, what is sacrifice in chess?"

"It is the offering of pieces to the opponent."

Salutati kept leafing through the pages.

"Sacrifice was particularly widespread in the Romantic age of chess," the professor answered, moving alongside him to have a look at the book. "But today it is no longer as popular."

"Why?"

"Because chess theory has become so sophisticated that it can predict all the various forms sacrifice can assume. To offer a piece to your enemy today would be nothing short of suicidal. Usually he will take advantage of it and win."

"I see."

"Very few masters still do it," the professor went on. "Most players choose not to risk. They prefer to win or, at the worst, to tie. It is a universal tendency. They don't want to lose."

"Of course," Salutati nodded.

He was weighing the book in his hand while looking elsewhere. Then he looked at the professor and hesitated:

"You know what just popped into my mind, for no reason? Daverio."

"Ah," the professor said, bowing his head.

"You know I can't get him off my mind? I always thought he would be likely to try it, but without success."

Squinting, the professor kept his eyes fixed onto the now sunny street. A puddle sparkled right in front of the bookstore.

"Do you remember what I told you about your elusive enemy?" Salutati asked him.

"Yes, I do."

"Obviously, he was the one. You needn't look any further."

The professor nodded. Silently, he adjusted his books one on top of the other.

"And yet," Salutati added. "To me, he looks like the victim."

He also turned toward the street. The pavement was rapidly drying up.

"Maybe because he is dead. But what about us?"

"What do you mean?" the professor muttered.

"He has preceded us, don't you think? He has only preceded us."

When the professor left the bookstore with Salutati, at closing time, the air had warmed up. At the end of the street, the sunset clouds formed an immense pink cumulus right above the Palazzo dei Congressi. The professor shook Salutati's hand and started walking down the sidewalk. As he reached the pedestrian crossing, he turned around and saw Salutati still standing where he had left him, in front of the bookstore, while the owner had already hooked the shutter and was pulling it down. He waved his hand at Salutati who raised his in response. Waiting for the traffic light to turn green, he fixed his wet eyes on the shimmering dome of the Palazzo. He tried to remember where he had read that when other people move us we are generally thinking of ourselves. Salutati kept gazing in his direction until the shadow of a bus eclipsed him.

The Eridanos Library

1. *Posthumous Papers of a Living Author,* by Robert Musil
2. *Hell Screen, Cogwheels, A Fool's Life,* by Ryunosuke Akutagawa
3. *Childhood of Nivasio Dolcemare,* by Alberto Savinio
4. *Nights as Day, Days as Night,* by Michel Leiris
5. *The Late Mattia Pascal,* by Luigi Pirandello
6. *The Waterfalls of Slunj,* by Heimito von Doderer
7. *The Plague-Sower,* by Gesualdo Bufalino
8. *Cold Tales,* by Virgilio Piñera
9. *The Baphomet,* by Pierre Klossowski
10. *The Invisible Player,* by Giuseppe Pontiggia
11. *Baron Bagge, Count Luna,* by Alexander Lernet-Holenia
12. *The Resurrection of Maltravers,* by Alexander Lernet-Holenia

Eridanos Press, Inc., P.O. Box 211, Hygiene, CO 80533.

*This book was printed in November of 1988 by*
*Il Poligrafico Piemontese P.PM. in Casale Monferrato, Italy.*
*The Type is Baskerville 12/14.*
*The paper is Corolla Book 120 grs. for the insides*
*and Acquerello Bianco 160 grs. for the jacket,*
*both manufactured by Cartiera Fedrigoni, Verona,*
*especially for this collection.*